Jubilee Rose

Karen J. Hasley

This is a work of fiction. The characters described herein are imaginary and are not intended to refer to living persons.

ISBN-13:978-1500744441
ISBN-10:1500744441

1868

Chapter 1

Lady Rose Carlisle, youngest child of Robert, Marquis of Symonton and his cherished wife, Claire, might have missed the entire appalling incident if she had not been trapped into conversation with The Honourable Oswald Sweete-Cotton. With anyone but Sweete-Cotton, Rose would have stayed focused on the speaker's face as he conversed—she had been raised to impeccable courtesy, after all—but with that particular acquaintance Rose knew she must anchor her attention on something other than the man himself.

Purposeful distraction was an absolute necessity on Rose's part because she felt the stirring of giggles at the base of her throat and knew from experience that the giggles would metamorphose into full-blown guffaws if she must continue to converse with Sweete-Cotton while simultaneously viewing his attire. Men were worse than women sometimes, and women were bad enough. Still, Rose was confident that even the most unstylish woman of her acquaintance had enough fashion sensibility not to wear checkered knickerbockers of a particularly awful shade of pea green with a dreadful velvet jacket in orange, all topped by a deerstalker hat. It was simply too much. Whatever had happened to plain blues and blacks and common sense kinds of colors? If that wasn't disastrous enough, he had that ridiculous monocle thing stuck in his eye and with those long sideburns and bristly mustache he looked exactly like a Cyclops rabbit, even to the overbite.

Rose heard Carmine clear her throat and recognized the tone. Carmine, who had known Rose for many years, realized her charge was on the verge of making an idiot of herself by breaking out into laughter usually considered too hearty to be feminine. Worse, she would be doing so on the fashionable thoroughfare of Regent Street, right outside the front door of the reputable shawl shop of Farmer and Rogers with all sorts of respectable people going in and out. Carmine, lady's maid par excellence, tried to head off what could turn out to be an(other) embarrassing incident for which her mistress would feel some chagrin later and gave another small, discreet cough.

Rose took a shaky breath and commented in a pleasant voice, "Yes, it is indeed a lovely day, Mr. Sweete-Cotton. After all the rain of this past week, I believe half the town is out and about on errands, which reminds me of several stops I have yet to make."

Sweete-Cotton, a young man of indifferent height and an unfortunate chin, did not take the hint. Instead, he gave the preening laugh he had practiced at home for just such an occasion as this and began to embellish her comment about the weather in a way that Rose found boring and nonsensical. Something about her being a rose made for sunshine and sure to embellish some fortunate man's garden and dare he hope that he might be permitted to call on her at her cousin's residence.

Rose shifted her weight from one foot to the other and lied with creditable courtesy, "I am afraid my cousin has been unwell and we are keeping a quiet house just now."

If you appear at my door, I will run shrieking through the halls, she thought. I could no more bear your tedious and self-serving conversation than an attack of the gout, but she said nothing of the sort and not a hint of it showed in her tone or expression. Lady Rose Carlisle did not take pleasure in unkindness, and she had been raised to exhibit courtesy to everyone she met, regardless of station or appearance or her own personal preferences. She was a young lady of quality where the word actually meant something.

Still trying to maintain her emotional equilibrium, Rose shifted her gaze past Sweete-Cotton's obviously padded shoulder to the street beyond and thus she saw it all.

A ragged boy darted out from the crowd with a man in shouting, furious pursuit and ran immediately into the path of a hansom cab. Its horse reared back and clipped the lad's head with flailing hooves and knocked him backwards. A sudden fount of bright red blood cascaded down the side of the boy's head and without a sound he dropped to the street into a limp heap of what could have been mistaken for a bundle of rags. The man that was chasing the boy stopped next to him and, frustrated that his quarry should choose such an unsporting way to elude him, gave the inert body a too rough nudge with the toe of his boot. It was that disdainful gesture that decided Rose's course of action.

She turned away from Sweete-Cotton right in the middle of some ridiculous comment he was making about the color of her eyes—a color he couldn't possibly know because Rose had not made direct eye contact with the man once during the entire, one-sided conversation—picked up her skirts and her pace, and forced her way through the gathering crowd to the unconscious boy's side.

Carmine, muttering a doomsday pronouncement under her breath, followed on Rose's heels. The maid knew exactly what was going to happen, could have written it out chapter and verse. Not that she minded all that much. Being personal attendant to Lady Rose Carlisle was absolutely the best position she had ever held in her entire life. It might be that the young lady had special ways about her, that she was high-spirited and strong-minded and sometimes hard to keep up with, but she was also good-natured and practical, never top-lofty or malicious, and more thoughtful to a servant than any employer Carmine had ever known. She'd follow her mistress straight into Bluegate Fields if needs be. Not that it had come to that yet, but with Miss Rose there was no way of knowing what she might take it in her mind to do tomorrow.

Rose crouched next to the boy in the street, tore off the pretty cummerbund around her waist, and pressed it against the bleeding wound on the boy's head before she turned a stern, unsmiling, dark-browed face to the man with the impatient foot.

"You, sir, would do well to control yourself and your offensive foot. The boy is unconscious so there is little opportunity for you to teach him a lesson right at the moment."

"The useless rapscallion stole from me. See. It dropped from his hand."

The *it* to which he referred was a cheerful cherry-red ribbon that fluttered on the pavement and looked like another stream of blood from the boy's head wound.

"A ribbon for a boy's life," Rose said, her voice so scornful that it penetrated the man's outrage. "Leave your card and I'll see that you are reimbursed for so precious a trifle. Now go away or I will find a pretense for having you arrested."

"Oh, Miss, your skirt's getting all stained." Carmine knew the comment would annoy her mistress but couldn't help herself. She had taken more than the usual time to see that Rose was dressed perfectly when they left this morning—really, her mistress was such a beautiful young lady when she put her mind to it—but now Lady Rose looked as she did when she was home and just returned from trudging through the rough and rocky terrain of Cornwall, hat crooked, hair coming loose from its pins, skirts stained and crumpled. Sometimes it made a person wonder why she even tried.

Rose shot Carmine the look the maid had expected, her lips pressed together unbecomingly and those dark brows furrowed over her eyes.

"Don't talk nonsense, Carmine. Pay that man something and make him go away." She turned her attention back to the boy, who had not stirred and whose face was pale as paper.

Behind Rose a man said, "Don't bother. I'll take care of it." Rose heard the jingle of coins, then the same man's voice saying, "This should more than compensate you for your loss." No scorn in his voice but a bland, well-bred tone with an undercurrent of warning that made the ribbon-seller clutch the coins and quickly disappear into the small crowd that had gathered.

"Everything is under control," the same man continued, apparently to the gathered onlookers, "and I very much fear you are disrupting traffic. May I suggest you all be on your way?" He had the kind of voice that assumed things would happen exactly as he intended and in this case they did. The little bustle of people that had been shuffling behind Rose disappeared.

Mr. Sweete-Cotton, who had eventually followed Rose after her abrupt departure, remained standing in the thoroughfare, uncomfortable with the situation and horrified at the sight of a Marquis's daughter kneeling in the street holding a filthy beggar boy against her skirts.

"I say, Lady Rose, this won't do. Won't do at all. Come away now."

Rose looked up long enough to tell him curtly, "I'll be just fine, Mr. Sweete-Cotton. There's no need for you to trouble yourself about me. Please do continue with your day."

To which Carmine added to no one in particular, "You might as well do as she says. I can tell by her expression that her mind's made up."

The man that had dispersed the crowd came and crouched next to Rose. "Let me see."

Rose, kneeling in the street with one hand acting as a cushion under the injured boy's head and the other pressing the now-sodden cloth against his injury, turned toward the voice. At first she saw only dark trousers and well-polished boots, but when the man gently pushed the cloth away so that he could view the wound, she met a gray-eyed gaze.

"It's all right," he said with a gentle tone, "I have no intention of abusing the lad further or arresting him. I'm a doctor."

Rose promptly forgot that Oswald Sweete-Cotton still stood there expecting a response from her, forgot that he existed on the planet at all, in fact. She moved aside, something in the doctor's voice causing her heart to beat uncommonly quickly for just a minute before it settled back into its regular rhythm. When she stood, Carmine began to brush at Rose's skirts.

"Carmine, we need to find a way to get the boy home." Rose, thinking through the next step, was oblivious to Carmine's fussing.

"Oh, Miss, you know that won't do here in town. Your cousin—"

"Yes, yes, I know, but there's no reason Alice need ever find out."

Carmine was poised to give the response such a ludicrous pronouncement deserved when the passenger in the interrupted hansom cab peered out over the folding door.

"Will he be all right?"

A petite, gray-haired, soft-voiced woman with a charming French accent looked at the scene in front of her, her expression and tone concerned. Rose had difficulty judging the woman's age. She could have been anywhere between forty and sixty, but the lines on her face, at the corners of her mouth, and around her eyes, bespoke if not greater age at least greater grief or suffering. The woman wore a dress of what looked to be fine gauge silk and a becoming hat with a delicate gauze veil over the upper half of her face so she obviously was not poor. Everything she wore was quite stylish but all in black, Rose noted, so perhaps the lines on her face were indeed from a recent grief.

The man answered, "I can't say. It's a nasty gash and may need stitches." That comment ended Rose's speculation of the French woman and brought her back to the crisis at hand.

"We can take him to my cousin's house on Pembroke Court. Carmine, where was Peek meeting us with the carriage? Go and tell—"

The woman in the cab said, "No, no. I can transport the child wherever he needs to be taken."

Rose never argued with the obvious and gave the driver of the cab her cousin's address. "That's an excellent idea. Doctor—" she paused and as the man picked up the boy's slight figure in his arms he supplied, "Merton."

"Dr. Merton," Rose continued, "it was so fateful that you appeared on the scene I can only think you will want to see this story through to its end. Unfortunately, I cannot imagine how we will all fit in this cab."

From the corner of her eye, Rose saw the gray-haired woman's arrested, almost frozen look as the man approached the cab carrying the injured child and hastily told her, "There's no need to be concerned, madam. It's a short journey and the lad's head is hardly bleeding at all now. If you would be so kind as to lend us this cab, you will be rid of us in short shrift."

The woman shifted back inside and pressed herself into a corner, one hand against the base of her throat as if she already regretted the offer. Rose climbed in beside her and when seated extended her arms for the child. The doctor hesitated.

"He's a bit of a mess, I'm afraid." The boy's clothes were grimy and blood-stained and overall he smelled of sweat and the streets.

"Nothing that won't wash off," Rose responded cheerfully. "I once got into a shoving match with my older brother in the stables at home and landed in a pile of something for which there is no delicate word or description. This is nothing compared to that lamentable occasion." The doctor gave her a quick, appreciative look and placed the boy on her lap.

Carmine, looking in at the motionless figure, commented, "He's awful still," eyeing the boy and wondering if they were carrying a corpse home. Now that *would* be hard to explain.

From the corner, the older woman made a weak-voiced observation. "I am a very small person and I believe we might fit the doctor in with us, but I do not believe there will be room for anyone else." Rose made an immediate decision.

"Carmine, you go and find Peek and tell him to take you straight home. And not a word to him about what's happened. His loyalties are too divided."

"You don't think he'll notice your absence, Miss?" asked Carmine dryly. "We did all depart from home together, you recall."

"Oh, you'll think of something, Carmine. Dust off one of your favorite excuses. Goodness knows you must have a repertoire by now. I'll meet you there. We need a plan."

Carmine looked at the doctor, decided he was no threat to her young miss especially with the older woman present, and gave a sigh.

"Yes, Miss Rose, but I can't see how this is going to work."

"I always think of something," Rose assured her with a smile. "Now go. I'll be fine."

Dr. Merton, sitting at the very edge of the seat so there was more room for the women, placed two fingers at the base of the child's throat.

"He has a good, strong heartbeat and with the bleeding stopped he may not need stitches after all. He'll have a powerful headache, though, and will need to stay quiet and observed for a day or two."

"That won't be a problem." Rose's tone was confident and almost breezy, but her eyebrows drew together again. To the doctor she looked deep in thought and not quite as confident as her tone would have him believe. Then her expression cleared and she raised her remarkable eyes to his.

He had noticed her eyes briefly earlier and now, closer, they were even more magnificent than he'd first thought, clear and a light sky blue with the pupils rimmed with just a hint of deeper blue. Their effect was a striking contrast to her dark, chestnut hair and brows, and against a complexion that was as becomingly flushed as her name. Certainly not the fair winsomeness that was so popular in all the young misses he had had the misfortune to meet this season and nothing like the golden hair of his dreams but vibrantly attractive nevertheless.

"I've forgotten my manners in all the activity. I'm Rose Carlisle." She had a straightforward smile with nothing shy or hesitant about her.

From the corner the petite Frenchwoman spoke. "And this is Dr. Merton as I heard. I am the Baroness Juliana de Anselme. Despite the misfortune of the occasion, I am happy to make your acquaintance." The French accent made her English lilting, almost musical. "You are quite certain, Doctor, that the child will recover."

"Yes, quite certain, barring anything extraordinary."

"I am much relieved. I have been in England only a week and in London just a day. I would hate to begin my stay under the weight of the death of a child." Behind the veil her face turned sad and her voice lost some of its music. "My husband recently died and I am traveling for a change of scenery. To try to escape death and then nearly cause it in one so young would have been unbearable."

"I'm sorry for your loss," the doctor said. His response was reflexive but sounded sincere, nevertheless.

Rose, seldom at a loss for words and almost always sure to say the right if not the expected or common thing, told the Baroness, "The boy came rushing pell-mell out of the crowd and directly into the path of the horse. There is no way you or your driver is accountable for any of what happened. Indeed, your generosity in allowing us to inconvenience you this way says you are both kind-hearted and responsible." The Baroness smiled at that.

"I do not think I am either of those things, but I will not argue the point."

It stayed quiet for a while, all three of them crowded together and the boy—much too slight, Rose thought, with a sharp little face and his arms and legs like match sticks—slumped with his head against her breast.

Finally, Rose spoke. "There may be a small matter, hardly worth mentioning, really, of getting the boy into the house."

Dr. Merton, who had been waiting for some such admission, only turned his head to look at her, brows raised slightly, the picture of polite interest. For a large man squeezed into a small space, he didn't look in the least uncomfortable or inconvenienced.

When neither of her companions asked for additional information, Rose continued, "I am in town visiting my cousin Alice, you see, who is really a very nice woman. A very kind woman, also, I would add, but I have always thought, in the most affectionate way possible, that she has a tendency to put too much store in the proprieties. Alice is very routine." As an afterthought she tacked on, "I call her routine in the most affectionate way possible, of course."

The doctor's lips twitched briefly before he asked, "Are we to assume that your cousin may protest admitting this boy into her home?"

"She may experience some hesitation, some very slight hesitation, which is why it would be in her best interest were I able to broach the subject to her over time, over a specific length of time, gradually, you understand, so as not to alarm her. She is rather a fluttering sort of woman."

"But fluttering in the most affectionate way possible, I'm sure."

Rose's gaze flew to the doctor's eyes, but she found only a bland interest there. Her own eyes narrowed as she looked at him. He was too smooth by half and for just a moment she would have sworn he was having her on.

After a moment she answered with agreeable good humor, "Oh, absolutely. I'm very fond of my cousin Alice and I am convinced that she will eventually see how sensible it is to use some of the room in that great house we currently rattle around in to allow this young scamp to regain his health. It is only the two of us there, you know, Alice and I and the army of servants that apparently two women must have to lead a comfortable life. That's where the problem lies, you see."

"I'm afraid I do not see," the Baroness admitted, "but perhaps it is my English that is at fault."

"No, Baroness," the doctor said. "My English is quite respectable and I do not see, either."

"A few of the staff, not many but enough to be troublesome, believe that I cause too much of a stir in the house, and they disapprove of nearly everything I say or do," explained Rose.

"Preposterous."

At that pronouncement she shot another look at the doctor and almost surprised a laugh lurking in his gray eyes despite his soberly outraged tone.

"I agree, Dr. Merton, quite preposterous, but there is no accounting for some people's perceptions. Forsythe, my cousin's butler, is the most vocal in his disapproval of my conduct so you can see that it would be much better if we were to stop some distance from the house and not directly in front."

"I am sorry for being so dense but I still don't see." The doctor again, clearly apologetic for his thick-headedness.

"I'll explain in a minute but please ask the driver to pull to the side right here." Dr. Merton, intrigued, did so and then turned as much as he could in the crowded cab to look at Rose as she continued. "Forsythe does not play fairly. My cousin Alice is a tractable and mild woman unless she feels something may reflect on her husband, my cousin Mayhew. Mayhew is in the diplomatic service and as long as I can remember has feared the effects of scandal on his career. The idea is especially ludicrous because Alice is a very sweet and proper woman who couldn't do anything scandalous if she set her mind to it."

"Unlike you."

"Well, yes, I suppose that's true, but I visit only once a year and I do try to maintain the proprieties when I'm here. There was that one little incident with the milliner's assistant but that was hardly my fault, and I would do it again despite the scolding I took. That poor child was so fatigued she—well, I digress. My point is that if I attempt to bring this boy in through the front door, Forsythe will kick up a fuss. He will run to Alice and tell her that it's the action of a progressive and Sir Mayhew would never approve. Not that Mayhew will even be home for the next month, but that won't matter. Forsythe will natter on and Alice will then feel compelled to take a stand and refuse in her apologetic way to let the boy in."

"Forsythe is a devil," said Dr. Merton vehemently, and this time the laughter was clear in his eyes. Rose met his look with an unfeminine grin of her own.

"A little too strong, Doctor, but he is old and set in his ways, quite immoveable and terribly conservative, so the thing is to get this young man inside without Forsythe knowing. We need a diversionary tactic." Rose turned her blue eyes on the Baroness.

"I have been many things in my life but never a diversionary tactic," that woman said. "I cannot imagine that I am fit for such a task."

"But you are, you know. You're perfect."

"You are too kind." The Baroness was smiling, too. There was something so very engaging about this young woman with her hat askew, a smudge of dirt across her chin, and a ragamuffin boy held firmly in her lap setting forth her plan with all the seriousness of a military general. She had not felt so light-hearted for many, many months, not since Pierre had come into her bedchamber and met her look in the glass there and told her he was ill. She had not been able to feel happiness or whimsy or delight or anything besides grief and fear through all the months of losing him, and it was a relief to want to smile at the sight of this Miss Carlisle and her crooked hat and her fine eyes and the no doubt ridiculous plan she was hatching.

"I am at your disposal," the Baroness said finally. "I shall be the finest diversionary tactic it is possible to be."

Rose smiled her approval and explained her plan and everyone's role in it. Her audience, either overcome with admiration for the plan's tactical brilliance or simply overcome, acquiesced without protest or question.

As Dr. Merton stepped out of the cab and took the still unconscious boy from Rose, she turned to give the Baroness a sparkling look before she followed the doctor down the street.

"I have every confidence in you, Baroness. You are French, after all, and the French are much better at distractions than the English. We are too conventional for our own good."

Chapter 2

None of the plans Dr. John Merton had considered for the afternoon included creeping in through the kitchen door of a large house on Pembroke Court and carrying an unconscious child up to the second story via the servants' staircase. Yet here he was following Rose Carlisle, who ascended the stairs with nonchalant confidence as if she had done it before. From what he had seen of her, he guessed she most likely had. Perhaps she made a habit of it for exercise or for some diversion of her own that suited her unconventional personality because she never hesitated but took the steps quickly. He climbed more slowly, a broad-shouldered man, not hulking but tall so that the staircase was a narrow fit for him, especially with the burden of the boy in his arms.

Upon first entering the kitchen they had passed a stocky cook that looked up slightly startled at their entrance until she saw Rose with a finger pressed to her lips. Then the cook gave a shrug and went back to her bread dough, a parade through her kitchen apparently nothing out of the ordinary. Dr. Merton thought his own cook might have reacted with more energy, but then she would have been naturally surprised at similar visitors in her kitchen. Neither he nor his guests were in the habit of spending a great deal of time in the scullery, unlike Miss Carlisle, who seemed to find her way along back passageways with casual poise.

As they came through the door onto the second floor landing, Rose stopped for a minute to brush back the child's hair and say with a slightly worried air, "You're very sure he's all right? He seems so still and pale, poor boy, and awfully thin to take such a blow."

"He'll recover from the blow to his head, but I can't say the same for the long term effects of poor nutrition and climbing into chimneys."

"He is a sweep, then? I thought he might be."

"Oh yes," the doctor said with grim assurance. "His sleeve slipped up and gave me a glimpse of one elbow. He's a sweep."

"Well, we need to get him better and then decide what to do with him. I have no intention of sending him back to that kind of life."

They were speaking in low voices near the top of the stairs when they heard from the front door below the muted but accented voice of a woman.

The Baroness had arrived, handing Forsythe her card, no doubt, and asking for Miss Carlisle in a friendly manner. "My new friend," the Baroness explained, "is such a charming young lady and so kind to invite me to call."

Rose gave the doctor a shove into the nearest room.

"Put the boy in here, doctor. Then can you find your way back down by yourself? Give me at least five minutes before you appear at the front door. Oh, good, here's Carmine." The maid stepped into the chamber and waited for direction. "Carmine, watch our young guest here until I return." Rose gave the doctor another shove, this time out of the room. "There you go, Dr. Merton. You must disappear back down the stairs and around to the front door while I change this dress and do something with my hair before Forsythe sends someone to tell me I have a caller below."

The doctor, unused to being pushed in and out of rooms in so nonchalant a manner, found he had unexpected patience with the imperatives.

"Yes, of course," he said. "Which part of the plan is this again?"

"The double frontal attack," Rose told him, a gurgle of laughter emerging from her throat. "Now go, and don't look at me like that. I know exactly what I'm doing."

As he hurried back down the stairs, through the kitchen and once more past the cook—his appearance did not warrant even a sidelong glance from the woman this time—out into the kitchen garden, and around the side of the house, Dr. Merton found that he believed his commander. If ever there was a woman who knew exactly what she was doing, it was Miss Rose Carlisle.

The front door was closed and when it opened to the doctor's ring, the Baroness still stood just inside regaling Forsythe with enough nonsensical chatter to give the doctor time to appear and Rose the opportunity to make herself presentable. Forsythe was a short, rotund man with heavy sideburns that almost joined at his chin and eyes, eyes that usually appeared too small for his face except when he was surprised by something as unexpected as the presence of Dr. John Merton at his front door. Forsythe's eyes certainly widened at that.

"Your grace," he said and stood there staring at his guest. Then he recollected himself enough to add, "I'm afraid Sir Mayhew is away for the season."

Dr. Merton, surprised that the butler recognized him, stepped inside and said amiably, "How fortuitous, then, that I have not come to visit Farmington. I have come to refresh my acquaintance with his charming cousin, Miss Carlisle."

"Lady Rose?" Merton did not blink at the subtle correction.

"Yes, of course, Lady Rose. And is it my friend the Baroness that I see here as well?" He strode forward, handing his hat to the butler with a casual gesture and taking the Baroness's hands in both his own as if he had not seen her since the Revolution. "Baroness, what a pleasant surprise to find you here! You are well, I hope."

"How kind of your grace to inquire. I am quite well and anticipating the lively company of my dear friend, Lady Rose. How remarkable that we should both pick this particular time to visit her!"

"Positively uncanny," Merton agreed. He proceeded to engage the Baroness in inconsequential conversation until Forsythe, finally recovering from the shock of two such impressive personages appearing at his door, began to apologize.

"I am very sorry to have to tell you that Lady Rose went out this morning and has not yet returned. I'm sure she will be devastated to have missed your visits."

There was a brief anticipatory pause until from the stairs behind them Rose said, "Oh, is it Baroness de Anselme? How delightful! And Dr. Merton, as well? Like Portia, I am twice blessed." She swept down the stairs resplendent in a dress of ecru silk with a high necked Fichu La Valiere over her shoulders in a pretty shade of rose that made her natural cheek and lip color even more vivid. Her gleaming hair was pulled back and fell in ringlets against one shoulder. She looked nothing like the young woman of smudged face who had sat in a blood-stained dress holding a dirty boy in her lap. "But, of course, I'm here, Forsythe. I thought you heard us come in." She turned innocent eyes on the butler, who at the last minute stopped himself from scowling at her.

"No, Lady Rose, I did not hear you come in and I cannot imagine how I missed you. I was here all the while."

"I can't imagine, either. Perhaps you stepped down to the kitchen, however briefly. Has my cousin returned yet?"

"I did not step down to the kitchen and Lady Alice is still out. At least, I think she is."

"Oh, dear, then she shall miss our guests and I know that will disappoint her. Please arrange tea for the Baroness and the doctor and myself and be sure to include some of cook's delectable ginger biscuits."

"I would be pleased to offer tea to the Baroness and his grace." Forsythe said the last two words deliberately in a tone intended to chastise Rose for her choice of words. Rose was discomfited for the briefest of moments.

"His grace?" she asked blankly before catching herself and repeating, "Of course, his grace," in a confident tone that said she had known all along that she was dragging a peer of the realm up the servants' staircase. John had to admire her ability to recover.

Even with Forsythe well out of earshot once they entered the parlor, the Baroness still lowered her voice to ask, "All is well, I trust?"

"Very well," Rose told her warmly. "Carmine is standing watch and since my cousin Alice never goes to the north wing and thus Forsythe has no call to go there, either, I believe we will be able to let the boy lie low until he's strong again. It's fortunate I'm known for my prodigious appetite because that will allow me to ask for snacks at various and numerous times without arousing suspicion. We'll fatten that boy up so much he won't be recognizable by the time he's well enough to leave, although I'll have to put my mind to considering what exactly to do with him when that happens. Grandfather has said he absolutely cannot fit even one more at Loden Hall. I suppose I could ship him home to Cornwall as long as he got there before my parents returned from their trip. I know Papa meant it when he said not another one, but I don't believe he'd have the heart to send the boy away if he was already settled in before Papa and Mother got home." Without giving either of her hearers a chance to question this odd speech, Rose turned her attention to the doctor and asked, "And why, pray tell, am I addressing you as your grace? I thought you were a doctor."

"I am a doctor and a surgeon. Unfortunately, and more of a bother than anything else, I am also John, the fifth Duke of Quill and an assortment of other titles I tend to confuse or forget. I'm very sorry." He looked penitent and sheepish and a little embarrassed by the attention.

"You are *that* Dr. Merton?"

"As far as I know, I am the only Dr. Merton so I must assume I am also *that* Dr. Merton. Is it a bad thing?"

"Oh, no, not if you're the Dr. Merton that published scathing comments about corsets and designed one that fell from the shoulders instead of the waist." Rose spoke about lady's undergarments without a blush. "Are you that Dr. Merton?"

"Yes." He had expected some comment about his title, not his publications, and was taken aback.

"What an honor! I am delighted to meet you! I must say I found your ideas eminently sensible, which is why, of course, they won't take at all. We women are simply not allowed to be sensible."

"And you are *Lady* Rose Carlisle?"

"It is an afternoon of surprises, isn't it? My father is Robert, Marquis of Symonton."

"And your mother was a Penwarren."

"Yes. How do you know that? Cornwall is quite a distance and my parents don't spend much time in town. My father would tolerate the rigors of society only if it pleased my mother and Mother is happy anywhere Papa is, so London never figured much into their plans. I can't imagine that your paths ever crossed."

"Your Aunt Abby is cousin to my cousins. I attended William's and Abby's wedding."

"I was there, too, but I don't recall seeing you." Rose eyed him with a speculative look in her eyes, sure she would have remembered such a well-proportioned figure or that head of black hair. He was quite a distinctive looking man, duke or doctor, handsome in a way that was refreshingly masculine, needing no padded shoulders or shoe lifts, a man to turn heads and not notice or care that he did so. There was something distinguished about the way he carried himself, that and the wide-browed face both possessed a certain nobility completely apart from his title. Rose decided that she liked him in spite of his being a duke and would not hold his birth against him. It was no more his fault than hers for being born into the peerage. As he said, it was a bother sometimes, but what could they do about it but tolerate the inconvenience?

"I don't recall seeing you either, but that could be because it was twelve years ago and I imagine both of us have changed in the interim."

The Baroness, who observed this exchange of information wordlessly, asked, "But are you both related to the exploring Penwarrens? How exciting! I have read everything they have published, and it is as if I am there with them. So very stirring! I am sure it is the closest I shall ever get to finding a snake coiled next to me on the pillow. Which I admit is the way I like it. So much more comfortable to be curled up in front of the fire reading about the polar regions than actually to be there, don't you think?"

That caused a laugh and a quick retort from Rose, who wasn't quite as sure as the Baroness that reading about adventure was better than experiencing it. John joined in, too, taking the opposite position from Rose just on general principle. When the doors opened and the tea tray arrived, all three of them were in an animated discussion about the nature of adventure.

Rose was pouring tea and handing around plates of small sandwiches when she heard voices in the hallway.

"I believe my cousin Alice has arrived home."

"The cousin for which you have such affectionate regard?" John asked in a way that made the Baroness smile and Rose giggle in an undignified manner.

"The very same, and as much as I have enjoyed both of your companies I'm afraid I must ask you both to leave. I know, I know, a baroness and a duke, whatever can I be thinking? But if Cousin Alice finds you here and begins to flutter, we will never escape and I must return to our patient upstairs. I am so very sorry, truly. You may take a sandwich with you if you'd like, your grace. Tuck one into a pocket along with a cream cake. No one will notice."

John, the fifth Duke of Quill, was unused to being teased in quite so shameless a manner and had to swallow a laugh before he turned toward the woman that entered the room. Alice Farmington was short and plump and bore no resemblance to her cousin Rose except in her sincere friendliness.

"My goodness, we have guests. How do you do? Your grace, we met at a reception last fall at the home of the Pendeckers, but I don't expect you will remember meeting me. There was such a press of people in attendance, all there to hear your cousin Chloe play the pianoforte. Such a talented young woman, I must say. How she could remember all that emotional Beethoven, I am sure I don't know. Just listening to his pieces always makes me feel quite fatigued, and it would be understandable if your cousin had collapsed in a heap on the floor after finishing that stirring sonata she played. Not that she did collapse, of course. Goodness, no, that would have caused a stir."

Rose was right on target, John thought, the woman does flutter, in the nicest, most affectionate way possible, of course, but definitely a flutter.

Rose introduced her cousin to the Baroness and immediately followed up by saying, "What unfortunate timing, cousin! The Baroness and his grace are just leaving."

"Oh, surely not. Can you not stay a while longer? We so seldom have company, except for Rose's gentlemen callers, of course, and they usually don't come more than once." Rose ignored that rather mystifying statement and gently, insistently put a hand on each of her new friends' arms.

"Such a pity, cousin, but his grace was just saying he was on his way to hear a presentation about lumbago."

At Alice's questioning look, John found himself explaining, "At the Royal Medical Society. A new breakthrough treatment. The medical community is talking about nothing else."

"This is the first I've heard of it," mused Alice, "and lumbago does run in our family. I'll mention it to Dr. Billet when I see him next. You must plan a return visit and share more information about the new treatment with us." By then they were out in the hallway and Forsythe was handing John his hat and reaching to open the door.

Rose was gracious in farewell. "Such an unexpected treat to have you both here on the same afternoon, and I am so sorry you must rush off like this. Please, please do say you will both return for another visit."

"How kind of you to ask and, of course, you are welcome to visit me at the Savoy where I am lodging temporarily. I apologize for my hasty departure, but my business man of affairs cannot be kept waiting," said the Baroness. "There are so many details to be discussed about my late husband's dealings on this side of the Channel that it will take several afternoons."

Her comments had the desired effect, silencing Alice's enthusiasms and causing her to say to the Baroness, "I am so sorry, Baroness, I didn't realize. Such a sad time for you."

"How kind," the Baroness murmured, and stepped out the front door where the cab waited at the curb. She descended the steps with the duke, her hand resting very lightly on his arm as the door closed behind them.

When the Baroness offered John a ride, he answered with a smile, "Thank you, but I need the walk to recover. I feel like Elijah must have felt swept up to heaven in the whirlwind."

"Yes, I understand. I remain breathless myself. It has been a pleasure being caught up in an adventure with you, your grace, and now I encourage you to return home quickly and study the lumbago. I cannot believe you have heard the last of that." The French lilt to her English was very pronounced and charming.

"I fear you're right and hope I haven't unwittingly started a medical rumor. Good afternoon, Baroness. I couldn't have had a more practiced conspirator, and I assure you the pleasure has been all mine."

He tipped his hat to her with a flourish and a grin, and she watched him walk away with a long stride and an athletic spring to his step. Only when he turned the corner and was completely out of sight did she direct the driver to her hotel, her original destination of several hours before. So much had happened in the meanwhile that it was unbelievable, the Baroness mused as she rode back to the hotel. Improbable and remarkable and quite unbelievable.

As soon as the door closed on their guests, Alice turned to her cousin and said, "My dear Rose, you never cease to amaze me. Where ever did you meet the Baroness de Anselme? She seems charming but I admit I know nothing of her."

"She has been in town only a day, Alice. I met her at Farmer and Rogers earlier today and liked her immediately. She seemed both brave and sad to me, and I invited her to visit, more to offer her my company than for any other reason. She was very grateful and arrived so quickly that I think she must be feeling rather lonely. I was glad I extended the invitation."

"But do you know anything about her, Rose, dear? Her family, I mean, or her situation?" Rose linked an arm with her cousin and walked her back into the sitting room.

"An ax murderer I believe she said, looking for her next victim. Oh, no, forgive me, I have her confused with the duke. He's the ax murderer. She is a grave robber." Alice tried to look offended, failed, and laughed instead.

"It's all very well for you to mock me, but with your penchant for bringing home strangers with unsavory pasts, I had to ask. Not that I'd mind about the Duke of Quill, even if he were an ax murderer. He is known to be so unsociable that to come home and find him in my front room nearly caused me palpitations. When did your paths cross?"

"There is the association with Uncle William and Aunt Abby, remember. He was at their wedding and so was I."

"But you were all of twelve years old, Rose."

"Yes, but a very mature twelve and possessed of a strongly retentive memory, so when I saw him again, I couldn't help but mention our connection."

"Rose, you were careful how you approached him, weren't you? I once heard him give a blighting set down to Amelia Struthers in the most offhand way one can imagine, and I wouldn't want you to be subjected to that, not that I think you're anything like that tiresome girl. To think she married into the Blanchett-Poores. I can hardly credit it. She'll breed those pale eyelashes of hers into the next generation."

Rose, who had thought Dr. John Merton, fifth Duke of Quill, to be good-humored, kind, and remarkably tolerant, was curious.

"We met on Regent Street," said Rose, careful with the facts, "and I did nothing indiscreet." She crossed her fingers when she said the latter, although surely the truth of the sentence was determined by how one defined discretion. "Whatever did Miss Struthers say to elicit an unhandsome set down from his grace? He seems so even tempered, I can't imagine it."

"She approached him dressed in Ottoman Velvet the color of straw, as I recall, which was her first miscalculation, fluttered those unfortunately pale eyelashes at him and told him how very noble and good she thought he was to treat the poor miserable creatures of the East End. Then she gave a small, artificial shudder and put her hand to her lips as if the idea were so unpleasant it was making her dyspeptic. His grace looked at her without speaking so long and so intently that she began to blotch. Finally, in a calm voice he said, 'You are a walking testimony, madam, for the necessity of formally educating women, particularly in the sciences. The most cursory lesson in biology would clarify that I do not treat creatures. I am a medical doctor. I treat people.' Then he walked away from her at a leisurely pace leaving poor Miss Struthers standing there with a look on her face that said *whatever is he talking about?* as clearly as if she'd spoken the words aloud. She is a trifle dim, I'm afraid. I was almost embarrassed for her, but you know her father once made some very unkind comments about my husband, unkind and undeserved, and I think the resemblance between father and daughter cannot be ignored."

"*Does* his grace treat the East End poor?"

"Rumor says so but I really have no idea. As I mentioned, he's rather unsociable and certainly a private man, which isn't to be wondered at, I suppose, considering."

Rose had seated her cousin and was in the process of bringing her a cup of tepid tea.

"Considering what?"

"His father, his upbringing, you know."

"No, I don't know. Tell me." She sat down next to Alice on the settee, shifted slightly so that she could curl one leg comfortably under her, and turned that bright blue gaze on her cousin. Alice could not resist the insistent curiosity of that look.

"Well, I suppose it's not really gossip any longer since it's been over twenty years and it really did happen. I'm only stating facts."

"What really did happen?" Rose at her most patient smiled and waited.

"I was new to town then and awed by everything, but there was no doubt that his grace's mother was the most beautiful young woman I'd ever seen. She was a true diamond, the only child of older parents and an heiress, besides being gorgeous with piles of black hair, dark eyes, skin like cream, and a figure to envy. Very charming, capricious, and willful, too, I recall, but then she was so young and full of life. We didn't often move in the same circles, but on those occasions when I saw her I was reminded of a brilliant butterfly, flitting from flower to flower. All the men were wild about her. I always felt grateful that I had come out the season before or even Mayhew might have been smitten."

The idea of stolid Mayhew with his practical nature and unimaginative temperament being besotted by any young woman, even the beauty her cousin had described, made Rose smile to herself.

Alice, catching the smile, said a little stiffly, "We were young once, too, you know, Rose."

Her comment troubled Rose's conscience and she leaned forward to say, "I was only smiling at the idea of Mayhew being smitten by anyone except you, cousin. It's clear he has eyes for no one else."

Mollified, Alice continued, "It was the buzz of the season when Anna accepted Leo, the fourth Duke of Quill's proposal.

No one could believe it. He had to be at least fifteen years her senior, a conservative and humorless man, but attractive in a dark and daunting sort of way and, of course, embarrassingly rich. They made a striking couple, but I told Mayhew from the start that it was not a good match. Her parents wanted it and she seemed willing—I don't think she went to the altar in tears—but I believe there were enough tears following the nuptials, poor girl. She was just eighteen, if that, and so gay. It must have been very difficult for her."

"He wasn't unkind to her?" Muted outrage in Rose's tone.

"Unkind? Not in the way you mean, not a brute, but he had no light or warmth about him, and I think she began to die a little from the very beginning. She had a son within a year, which is what despite everything made her actions so deplorable to me. I was a young mother myself and even if Mayhew had beaten me, which, of course, he never did nor ever gave such a dreadful action a thought but even if he had, I could never have left my children."

Rose followed the confusing sentence enough to ask, "The duchess left?"

"Young John must have been around nine when his mother ran off with the boy's tutor."

"No! She ran away with another man?!"

"Oh, yes. It was quite a scandal, let me tell you, and while I quite understand that her life must have been miserable, how she could abandon her son and leave him in that great, dark house with his embittered father is quite beyond me. I think it almost unforgivable."

Rose, who had an exaggerated sense of empathy and a lively imagination, did not feel so condemnatory. She thought it must have been like shutting a beautiful flowering plant in a closet so that it withered and died inch by inch. For her the wonder was that the Duchess lasted as long as she did.

"Poor boy," was all she said.

"Yes, poor boy, indeed. There was a quiet divorce and young John was shipped off to school and forbidden to speak of his mother or at least that's what the gossips said. He was a solitary child rattling around in that big house when he was home, and if his young cousins Chloe and Augustus hadn't moved in with him and his father in the spring of '56, I don't know what would have become of him."

"Aunt Abby was there, too, wasn't she?"

"Yes, and I recall a little rumor at the time that she might become the young Marquis's stepmother, but she up and married your Uncle William and began traipsing around the globe with him and that scotched the talk. Anyway, young John and his father got on better in the duke's later years and while at first I don't think he was at all pleased that his son was going into medicine, he became quite proud of him there at the end. I tell you, remembering how distant they were for such a long time, it nearly brought tears to my eyes to hear the pride in the old duke's voice when he introduced his son to Mayhew as *Doctor* Merton. Even Mayhew commented on how the older man had mellowed. Well, it's a blessing they reconciled because John ascended to the title not a year later from that meeting."

The story ended, Rose sat in silence. It had made an impression on her sensitive nature, the picture of a beautiful young woman in an unhappy marriage, a lonely little boy forsaken by both parents, really, and left to fend for himself in a world that was very often unkind to children. That made her remember the child upstairs, hopefully still sleeping under Carmine's watchful eye, and she stood up, dropping a kiss onto Alice's cheek.

"What a sad story! It makes me see his grace in quite a different light."

"Promise you won't tell him I gossiped so shamefully about him, Rose. I suppose I shouldn't have said anything but at least I stopped with his childhood. There was that mysterious episode with Penelope Carstairs a few years ago that started up the gossipmongers again."

"Penelope Carstairs?"

"Yes, Lady Fountain."

"There were rumors about Dr. Merton and the wife of the Marquis of Fountain?" Such illicit conduct was hardly unheard of at their level of social status—perhaps at any level of social status, high or low—and Rose could not have said why the thought caused her a pang of some unidentifiable, nearly painful emotion, but it did. She decided to blame indigestion.

"She was plain Miss Penelope Egan then, but yes, as I recall, rumor already had her a duchess. Quill was obviously enamored of her and she seemed to reciprocate his feelings. There was never a formal declaration but everyone anticipated a betrothal announcement at any time. When it finally came out, though, it was to Fountain, not Quill. No one knew what to make of it. She was the bride of the season, all that yellow hair and pink skin, although I've heard she's gone plump in unexpected places. Quill was never a social man, but after that he became positively reclusive. But now I am indulging in old gossip and I draw the line." Alice pressed her lips together and looked resolved to maintain her silence.

"And very properly so." Rose made no more comment about the duke's love affair. "The picture of the solitary upbringing his grace must have endured makes me appreciate all the more my wonderful childhood and the fact that my parents can still be as embarrassing to be around as young lovers."

"Your parents were a love match, that's certain, and no one could have imagined your father would be so quickly and so happily domesticated. He was my uncle before he was your father, remember, and always a cool, formidable man before he met Claire. Of course, she changed that quickly enough." From the doorway, Rose laughed back at Alice.

"Mother will always have her way. Papa never had a chance and he knows it. Now I find I am in need of a rest. All this activity has tired me out. Are there plans for the evening?"

"We are invited to one of the Bennetts' *at homes*." At Rose's grimace, Alice added hastily, "Please come, Rose. I know the last one was tedious, but I have it on good authority that their daughter Melanie is not going to sing this time. They've invited a harpist, I understand, of whom I've heard only good things. It would be so pleasant for you to meet people your own age."

"Men, you mean, but I am four and twenty now, cousin, and have used up all my seasons. Happily, too, since you know I am not very good at making conversation with men, or women for that matter, whom I find either vain or vapid. You should have heard Oswald Sweete-Cotton prosing on at me today." Alice's kind face took on a wise expression.

"Oswald Sweete-Cotton is not for you, my dear, but I believe there is someone for everyone. Only if you don't make an effort to get out, how will you ever find him? It's not as if suitable young men show up magically in the middle of the street." For some reason unknown to Alice her comment made Rose laugh out loud.

"I'm sure you must be right," Rose finally said, "but I believe I will have to pass on the Bennetts this evening. Please make some suitable excuse for me and do have a good time yourself. I'm going to rest, then take supper upstairs in my room."

"I won't fuss about tonight, Rose, since I rather dread the Bennetts myself. It must be the fear of Melanie making an impromptu appearance. But promise me you will come with us to the theater tomorrow evening. Stephen has volunteered to escort us and Lydia is coming, too. It will be very enjoyable." Stephen was Alice's son and Lydia his wife, a new mother and her first time out in public since the birth of the baby.

"Yes, I promise. I've wanted to see the stage performance of *Uncle Tom's Cabin* ever since I read the book. I wouldn't miss it." Rose went out the door and upstairs, stepping into the room where Carmine sat in the rocking chair by the injured boy's bed, darning linens.

"He's restless," she told Rose, "and every once in a while he calls for his mother or for someone named Ernie. I've been bathing his forehead with lavender water and trying to get him to drink some tea, but he only fusses."

"That's to be expected." Rose pushed back his hair to look at the heavy bandage she'd hastily patched across his forehead. "The doctor was right. It doesn't appear to be bleeding any longer. You can go for a while, Carmine. I'll stay with him. Send me up some warm lemon water and a little broth and I'll see if I can get something into him. Will you check back in an hour or so?"

"Yes, Miss."

"Oh, and Carmine—"

"Yes, Miss?"

Rose gave the maid a smile that lit the room and immediately made everything worthwhile. All the worry and annoyance and aggravation Carmine had felt earlier in the afternoon disappeared from her memory. That clear-eyed, friendly, warm look was one of the many reasons Carmine would not have traded places with any other lady's maid in the kingdom.

"Thank you," Rose said with simple sincerity. "You were invaluable today. I know I am often a source of despair and frustration to you, and I appreciate that you tolerate my behaviors without a great deal of fuss. I'd be lost without you."

Carmine colored faintly. Rose made a habit of small unexpected moments like this, moments that made a usually competent Carmine feel nonplussed and speechless. She should be used to them by now, but they still took her by surprise and left her without a response. So she said only, "Yes, Miss," for a third time and slipped out the door.

Carmine was a pragmatic woman and had been a servant for many years, had seen everything and experienced some of the hard knocks of life, but at times like this she honestly felt she would willingly and happily die for her young lady.

Chapter 3

Rose shooed Carmine away when the maid reappeared later.

"I'll sit up with him through the night. I'm not in the least tired and Cousin Alice will be gone all evening. If you could just keep Forsythe out of the way, I'd be grateful. I'll ring if I need you."

Around midnight she thought she might have made a mistake and would have to rouse Carmine, after all. The feverish and restless boy kept throwing off his covers and trying to rise, surprisingly belligerent and strong for so thin a child. Rose had to kneel next to the bed and practically throw her whole weight across him to make him lie still. After a while the worst passed and he lay quietly again, eyes opened, trying to focus on her face.

"You ain't Mum."

"No, I'm not. I'm Rose. You must get better so we can find your mum and let her know you're all right."

"Where's Ernie?"

"Ernie will be here as soon as you get better."

"Promise?" He had nearly black eyes that blazed out of his pale face.

"Yes, I promise. When you get better, we'll find Ernie." She felt him relax under her hands.

"Well, that's all right, then," he said and fell into a fitful slumber. Rose herself slept on and off in the chair by the bed and when Carmine first poked her head in just before daybreak, she found both boy and lady sleeping soundly.

"You go get some sleep, Miss."

Rose, awakened by Carmine's entrance, placed a hand against the child's forehead and stood, stretching.

"I believe I will. He feels quite normal now, and I think his sleep is truly restful."

"Was it a bad night, Miss?"

"He misses his mum and Ernie and Evie, whoever and wherever they all are, but it wasn't a bad night, Carmine. I've had worse." With a last look at her patient, she went off to her own room to lie down and was asleep within a minute.

Refreshed and energized, Rose awoke a few hours later, called for hot water to bathe, recoiled her hair and donned a gown of soft yellow and softer blue plaid. The influence of the queen, she thought looking at the dress, plaid being so unbecoming to most women that only royal preference could make it fashionable. This particular pattern, however, was tolerable, spring like in its colors and not so garish a yellow that it clashed with the soft pink of Rose's skin. She came downstairs to the morning room where Alice was munching on toast and sipping coffee.

"There you are," Alice said looking up with a smile of relief. "I was beginning to worry. You really must have been tired from your outing yesterday, and that's not like you, Rose. You aren't coming down with something, are you? I'm sure I would never forgive myself if your parents returned to find you in a sick bed."

"I feel quite healthy, thank you, and just catching up from several late nights. How was your evening with the Bennetts?"

"I was so glad you weren't there for it was just as I feared. There was a harpist as promised but her only purpose was to accompany Melanie. Really, it was very unsporting of them to lure us all there with the promise of an accomplished harpist and then force us to sit through Melanie singing Scottish airs, all off key, the loch and the gloaming and, oh, you know. They're such mournful songs to start with, so dour really, but when sung by a young woman who is always just a little above or below the notes, they make one positively suicidal. The only bright spot was when Lady Cormagant nearly toppled off her chair and we had to suspend the music while she righted herself. I'm sure half the people in the room contemplated similar inelegancies. It's so sad when one is reduced to planning a gymnastic feat just to make it through the evening. You were wise to stay home, Rose. By the by, Mr. Sweete-Cotton was there and asked for you. He also said he was pleased to see me so recovered from my sick bed." Rose stopped with her coffee cup midway to her lips.

"Oh, dear. I suppose I should have warned you that you were ill and we have been spending quiet evenings at home with few visitors as you recuperate."

"I always like to know when I've been ill, Rose," Alice chided gently. "It allows me time to look suitably wan."

"I forgot. I'm sorry."

"It's all right. By the time I spoke with Mr. Sweete-Cotton, Melanie had finished her recital so I daresay I looked appropriately pale. He does seem quite enamored of you, though. I don't suppose you—" She received a full and unblinking look from Rose's blue eyes and sighed. "No, I suppose not, and I really can't blame you. His conversation is so practiced and his sense of fashion so, so—"

"Awful?" Rose suggested. "Deplorable? Horrible? Ghastly? Hideous?"

"Any of them would do, I suppose, and still be lacking." The two women, of one mind, smiled at each other across the table. "Now," Alice went on more briskly, "what does your day hold?"

"Since we plan such a riotous evening, I thought I would spend a quiet afternoon writing letters. Great Aunt Sophie is past ninety and still possesses an unquenchable curiosity about all our lives. Grandfather and your dear mama constantly anticipate that I will write about my engagement and imminent marriage and I am overdue to raise their hopes with the sight of an envelope showing my handwriting, and Constance has written so enthusiastically about my two nephews, I should be ashamed that I have not yet responded with requisite and proper admiration. Twins do run in the family and I must commend her on maintaining the tradition." Rose stood to drop a small wisp of a kiss onto her cousin's cheek. "You really are the best of cousins to tolerate my nonsense. What will you do today?"

"I'm off to find new gloves first and then I plan to spend some time with the Misses Blassingame."

Rose resisted a shudder, saying, "You are a wonderful human being, Alice, and I can only hope you receive the full and due reward for your patient kindness sooner rather than later. I don't mean to be unkind, but the Blassingame sisters do twitter so. Last time I saw them they were like two sparrows fluttering around me, admiring my hair and my gown and my hat and anything else that was visible."

"They are gently bred women of a particular generation who mean well, Rose." Alice's voice was gently reproving and her young cousin looked properly penitent.

"I know. Forgive me and forget I said anything. I was unkind and superior and I wish I could take it back. Please share my kindest regards with them."

"And you won't forget about tonight."

"Never!" This with a smile.

"What color will you wear?"

Rose looked at her cousin with a blank expression. "I haven't the slightest idea."

Alice, appearing somewhat sheepish, responded, "I'm wearing light burgundy against a darker burgundy and green plaid. I don't suppose you could find something that wouldn't clash, Rose."

"Oh, dear. Does that mean the scarlet taffeta will not do?" Rose asked, then laughed at the quickly hidden dismay on Alice's face. "Don't worry. I promise we will be able to sit next to each other without causing an aesthetic offense. Enjoy your afternoon."

Once upstairs, Rose stopped in the patient's room surprising a scene of struggle as Carmine tried to keep the boy in bed. He was equally as determined to rise. Carmine cast Rose a grateful look and said, panting a little from the exertion, "There now. Here's Lady Rose so you don't need to go in search of her. I told you she'd be here soon."

Rose came in quickly, shutting the door behind her and said in a brisk tone, "You get right back into that bed, young man. You do not have permission to rise." Something in her easy authority spoke to him and he stopped fussing, relaxed back against his pillow, and lay quietly with his eyes fixed on her.

"Don't know about no lady but the voice is the same. You said you was Rose. I remember. I heard you."

"Yes, I am certainly Rose and the lady part isn't important. What's your name?"

"Piper," he said and was quiet, looking suddenly exhausted. He had dark circles under his eyes and all his freckles stood out like spatters of dark brown paint on his cheeks.

"Well, Piper, you had an accident, and you are here to get better, so you must promise not to fuss but to rest and eat what's good for you so you can get your strength back. Will you promise to do that?"

Instead of answering her, he asked, "Is this the work house?" If Rose was surprised by the question, she didn't show it.

"Certainly not. This is my cousin's house on Pembroke Court."

"Is she your cousin?" He nodded toward Carmine, who gave a quick shake of her head before Rose could answer.

"That blow must have knocked common sense right out of your head, boy. Do I look like a cousin to a lady like Miss Rose? I'm Carmine and I help out in the house."

"Will you promise to rest and eat what's good for you, Piper?" Rose persisted.

His dark eyes fixed on her face for a long moment. Then it was obvious he had come to some sort of decision for he relaxed and said simply, "You ain't got a half bad face. I don't figure you'll be turning me over to the Rat Catcher anytime soon so I reckon I can stay a little while." To prove he could indeed condescend to prolong his visit, he immediately fell asleep.

Rose wrote letters much of the afternoon just as she had said, using a lap desk and sitting in the large chair next to Piper's bed. She finished one to her Great Aunt Sophie, one to her grandparents, and one to her sister Constance, exactly as she had planned, but she wrote a much briefer missal in advance of those three. That note was to his grace, Dr. John Merton, Duke of Quill. Addressing it made her grumble a little at the confusion of titles, but she finally cast caution to the winds, tried to use common sense, and assumed he would not stand on ceremony if she got the titles or the order wrong.

Rose was right in her assumption. Dr. John Merton, fifth Duke of Quill, paid no attention at all to the titles scrawled across the envelope. He was not a man who put much store in titles to start with. Like Rose, he had been raised with them abounding in friends and family, but he did not scorn them so much as ignore them. The doctor had just returned home from morning at his surgery and Rathbone, a long-time devoted servant of the family, brought him the sealed envelope with a handwriting on the front his grace did not recognize. Feminine, John thought, but still a dark scrawl with a peremptory look about it. Breaking the seal, he read the note, read it a second time, and found himself simultaneously shaking his head and laughing aloud. Rathbone stood quietly. If he was curious about the contents of the envelope, he gave no sign.

Looking up at the old retainer, John said, "My plans for the evening have changed, Rathbone. Tell cook I'll take a light, early supper in the library. Then send round to the Royal Olympic and get me one ticket for *Uncle Tom's Cabin* currently playing there. I have an appointment this afternoon but ask Bellevue to ready whatever is appropriate for an evening at the theater. I confess it's been so long since I've attended I am at a loss as to what to suggest but tell him no plaid. I draw the line at wearing plaid."

"Very good, your grace."

Rathbone watched John tuck the envelope into an inside pocket, thinking that he had not heard such a happy tone in his master's voice for several years. It was so welcome a sound that even if a lightskirt was the cause of the Duke's sudden amiability, the old man would swallow his displeasure. While the butler thought that idea unlikely, he had learned over the years not to be surprised by anything that happened in this house. He had once startled a rabbit in the east wing hallway and found a skeleton dangling in the then-marquis's room—"I need it for study," John had explained as if speaking to a simpleton—so he supposed, as far-fetched as it might be, his grace might have made the acquaintance of a practiced paramour and was planning a rendezvous at the theater. So be it. The sound of the duke's rich laugh was long overdue. Rathbone would worry about the motivation for it later.

The Duke of Quill's appearance at the Royal Olympic Theater that evening caused a stir of which he was completely unaware. He was not a man with a well-developed sense of his own importance and would have been amazed that his appearance anywhere was of interest to very many people. So it was that he made his way through the crowd of theater-goers, nodding a greeting to acquaintances, stopping infrequently for a personal word with someone more familiar, all the while oblivious to the muted groundswell of interest that followed him. Once seated, he scanned the boxes, found whom he sought, and gave a brief nod in that direction.

Rose, already seated and watching for the doctor's appearance, saw his tall, dark-haired figure long before he found her, then caught the nod in her direction and with a half-smile, bent her head decorously in return before she turned her attention back to her cousin's daughter-in-law, only half-listening to Lydia's description of her perfect new daughter. For all her bravado, Rose had not been certain the doctor would come and was relieved and inordinately pleased to see his arrival. At the first intermission she rose, taking Alice by the arm.

"Come along, cousin. I feel the need for a stroll."

Alice did not argue but stood saying, "I can well understand why. I hadn't expected it to be quite so intense a production. My nerves are frayed already. I hope I won't embarrass you by weeping in the second act." Rose patted her hand.

"Weep away, dear. It is an awful story, and if one could soothe one's sensibilities by saying it is only fiction, it wouldn't be quite so harrowing. Unfortunately, the Americans are still recovering from the internecine war fought over the same dreadful circumstances being played out on the stage this evening. So in a way the production is not simply fictional entertainment and we should all weep at the story."

By the end of her speech, Rose had maneuvered her cousin into the middle of the crowd of people and was surreptitiously looking about her. From behind them someone said her name and she turned, feigning surprise at the sight of John Merton.

"Your grace, what a pleasant surprise!"

"I agree, Lady Rose. I had no idea you had a taste for American history." He turned to Alice, manners perfect, to say, "How very nice to see you again, Lady Farmington! Are you enjoying the production?"

"Yes, but as Rose pointed out it doesn't seem quite proper to *enjoy* it, if you take my meaning."

"I believe I do."

There was an infinitesimal pause before Rose said brightly, "I find I am quite parched," and waited, but not for long.

"Then allow me to bring you both some lemonade. I believe I saw refreshments somewhere."

"I know exactly where they are," Rose replied in a helpful manner. "Cousin, you sit here and we will be right back with something cool."

"But I am not really thirsty—"

"You may not be thirsty now, of course, but when you begin weeping in the second act, you will be glad you replenished your supply of liquids. We wouldn't want you to become dehydrated, isn't that right, Doctor?" Rose shot him a mischievous glance.

"Quite right. Dehydration is especially bad for lumbago, you know." Rose swallowed a laugh and rested her hand lightly on his arm.

"Did you learn that at your recent symposium? Who would have imagined such a medical connection?" Rose added in a lowered voice as they walked away, "Very quick, your grace, but be careful. Cousin Alice will want to know details and then you may be pushed into a corner from which there is no escape. I warn you only for your own good. I hope you have had time to brush up on lumbago."

"Since prior to three o'clock today I did not anticipate an imminent meeting with your cousin, I fear I may be forced to make something up."

"I am convinced physicians are forced to do so more frequently than their patients realize." The doctor shot Rose a surprised but laughing look.

"Lady Rose, I assure you I do not make things up when it comes to medicine."

"No? How boring, then."

"Boring only in your world, I'm afraid. Many of us go through life without making anything up at all."

"I believe I could argue a case quite the opposite, especially regarding the people all around us," Rose said, "but I haven't the time. I appreciate your presence here this evening and hope you are not too outraged by my presumptuous behavior. I was wondering if you would mind being party to a slight deceit."

"*Another* deceit you mean, since I already have one deceit accomplished. Is it about our young patient?"

"Yes, who remains concealed above stairs from both my cousin Alice and more importantly from the twitching nose of Forsythe. The boy's name is Piper and he seems awfully weak to me. I don't know if it's normal or not and hoped you could find time to take a look at him."

"Yes, of course, but how—?" He paused, met her innocent, blue gaze, and said, "Forgive me, I wasn't thinking. No doubt you have a plan."

They walked slowly back through the crowds toward Alice deep in conversation, neither of them aware of the stir they caused among some of the theater's patrons that commented to each other what a handsome couple the pair made and didn't it make sense to see them together since they were both just the tiniest bit peculiar?

By the time they found Alice and handed over the lukewarm lemonade, John understood his part and had his instructions memorized. He found that with Lady Rose Carlisle there was very little for him to do but say *I see* and *of course* at the appropriate times. She really did seem to have everything thought out and under control.

The three made pleasant, desultory chatter until it was time to return for the next act.

Alice, rising, said, "I hope you will not be a stranger, your grace. I have so many questions about the lumbago and am comforted that you have become an expert in the condition."

"I wouldn't say expert," John said with a faint tinge of desperation in his voice.

"Nonsense," replied Rose. She turned back to the doctor with a slight smile. "I'm sure his grace is just being modest. Why don't you write down all your questions, Alice, and if the doctor graces us with his presence—" her eyes twinkled at her little joke "—you will be ready for him?" With those words the two women were folded into the crowd and lost to his sight.

For just a moment John had found Lady Rose Carlisle absolutely adorable. She wore something in a becoming shade of mauve that swept off her shoulders, her rich chestnut hair coiled at the back of her neck and pearls at her throat and on her ears. There was something so genuine about her, a smile without artifice and not an eyelash fluttered in flirtation, that it was hard to believe there was such convoluted planning going on behind that remarkably clear gaze but, of course, that was the surprise and the delight. A true Machiavelli lurked behind those blue eyes. It was as intriguing as it was disconcerting.

Later that evening, home and a good night wished to her cousin, Rose spent the remaining hours once more curled into the chair next to young Piper's bed. He slept a great deal and when he was awake, lay still with his dark eyes fixed on Rose's face in an unsettling way.

More than once she raised her eyes from her book to find him soberly watching her until she finally asked, "What are you looking at so seriously, Piper? Is there something smudged across my face?"

She meant it as a joke but she was beginning to realize he was not used to being light-hearted, and he never laughed. That seemed to her worse than anything else, worse even than the brine-soaked and roughened knees and elbows and the thin bones and softened teeth that bespoke an inadequate diet, all very bad, indeed. But that one so young should not know laughter seemed to her still worse.

He considered her question seriously before answering, "Ain't nothing on your face that shouldn't be there. It's a right nice face. Makes me think of Mum, is all. I remember her sitting just like you are now, all curled up. Looked like you, too, only not so filled out."

"If you tell me where she is, Piper, I'll find her and bring her here. I don't doubt she's worried."

"She's been gone over a year now. Fever took her. When I left she was there and when I come home she was gone. Dead, Ernie said, and that was that." His unemotional tone struck

Rose's tender heart, but she was not overly sentimental or easily given to tears.

"How old were you then?"

"Ernie says I was five. I don't rightly know when I was born but Ernie remembers."

"What about your father, Piper? Is that Ernie?"

Piper sent her an incredulous look that Rose was wise enough to recognize as an unvoiced *no* to her latter question.

"Our pa went to work in the mines and never come home. Mum said the mines killed him."

Rose processed that unembellished statement and finally asked, "Well, then, who is the Ernie you talk about so often?" But at that question, the boy's mouth pressed shut.

"I'm feeling powerful tired," he told her shutting his eyes, and while Rose could tell that at first he only pretended slumber, his breathing soon took on the deep, slow sound of true sleep.

Mysterious Ernie, Rose thought with curiosity. She loved a good puzzle and thought she would make uncovering who this Ernie was a bit of a game, but the game was over almost before it began.

Rose awoke from her curled and cramped position sometime after midnight knowing she had heard something and imagined at first that it was Carmine come to check on her. She stood up in the dark room, the moon's pale glow through the partly-curtained window the only illumination, and looked toward the door. She would have sworn she had heard it creak but no Carmine stood there. A glance at the bed showed Piper still sleeping soundly, one arm thrown across his forehead and a leg sticking out from under the covers. Such a serious little boy, Rose thought, and tenderly rearranged the covers over him and brushed back the hair from his forehead to inspect the bandaged wound.

"I expect you will live, young man," she said aloud, "but what I'm going to do with you I have not yet figured out."

She thought he would sleep through the remainder of the night and went to her own room to throw on a nightdress and try to reclaim some of the night for her own rest, but she couldn't sleep. Something bothered her, something intangible but still so real that eventually she rose, threw on a wrap and went back down the hallway to the room where she had left Piper. She knew she had heard the door scrape open earlier and if not Carmine, then who? Forsythe, perhaps, in his sneaky way or one of the upstairs maids, now full of excitement about the unannounced houseguest and ready to spread the story at daybreak?

When she pushed open the door, however, she realized it had been neither Forsythe nor one of the servants. Instead, a boy older and larger than Piper bent over the bed trying desperately to lift the smaller still sleeping boy in his arms. At Rose's entrance, the newcomer froze, looking like a wild animal caught in the hunter's sights, eyes wide and suddenly as immobile as a statue.

"Here," Rose said but gently, "what are you doing?"

The boy let Piper back down onto the bed with care and stood to face her, both hands clenched into fists at his sides. He had Piper's face only fuller and older, with the same sharp nose and sharper chin. Rose stepped into the room and closed the door behind her but kept her distance, watching a look of stubborn defiance narrow the lad's eyes and raise his chin.

"Hello, Ernie," she said. The words made him gape at her.

"How did you know that was me?"

"Your brother has called for you since he's been here and you look just like him. You don't have to be a genius to figure it out. How did you get in?" She hadn't moved and neither had he but her question brought a smug little smile to his face.

"Ain't no place can keep me out if I want to get in." He gave no more details and Rose did not ask.

Instead she invited, "Why don't you sit down and stay a while? Piper just recently fell asleep and he needs to rest. It wouldn't be good for him to be moved just yet. The doctor is coming to see him tomorrow and we'll know more then." The boy didn't sit.

"Will he be all right?"

"Yes, I expect so, but he took a bad blow to the head and I don't think he should partake of any vigorous activity until the doctor says it's all right." She came farther into the room and repeated, "You can sit there right next to him for whatever's left of the night if you'd like and all day besides, as long as you keep quiet. Having your brother here must remain a secret."

"What you got planned for him, then?" He had a belligerent and suspicious edge to his voice, the tone of an adult three times his age who had lived a troubled life.

"That's a good question and one we can talk about later when he's better, but I give you my word that I would never hurt him and that your presence in this house will be just as much a secret as Piper's." Rose met the boy's dark, skeptical look with a clear-eyed, unsmiling one of her own and waited for his response. After a suspended moment, he gave a shrug.

"All right, then, I'll stay a while, but what a lady like yourself is doing with the likes of us don't make no sense to me. Nobs don't spend no time worrying about them what does their dirty work. That's been my experience."

"Yes, I'm sorry to say that's been my experience, too. Since it's still the middle of the night, I can't arrange anything for you to eat right now without alarming the kitchen, but in the morning I'll have breakfast brought up for you and we'll see what the doctor says when he arrives. Can you sleep in the chair?" He nodded. "Good. I'm going back to bed. I'm just two doors down the hall on the same side. Come and knock if Piper awakens and you need me."

With her hand on the door knob, he finally responded. "Ain't you worried I'll pocket the silver and scarper?" That made her laugh.

"The silver in this place is so heavy you couldn't scarper with it if you tried but to answer your question, no, I'm not worried. You came for a different treasure all together, didn't you?"

He missed her meaning at first but finally caught it, and something shifted in his face and lightened his expression. For the first time he looked like a boy. Eleven at the most, Rose thought, but like Piper he might be small for his age.

Ernie didn't answer her, just gave an abrupt nod and stood, watching her and still on guard until she pulled the door closed behind her. Two of them now, Rose thought on her way back to bed, and finding a home for one was challenging enough. Well, she'd worry about it in the morning. She was very good at sorting things out and making things happen, and she didn't know why this should be different from any of the other times. All she needed was a plan.

Chapter 4

Carmine awoke Rose early, knocking gently on the door and stepping inside her bedroom with a large pitcher of hot water in one hand.

"Oh Miss, you won't believe—"

"What?" replied Rose. She propped herself up on one elbow and looked at her maid. "That we now have two stowaways hiding out in the guest wing?" Carmine, open-mouthed and staring, stopped in the middle of pouring the hot water into the basin.

"However did you know that?"

"I see all; I know all," said Rose, waving her hand as she had once seen a magician do before she laughed and explained the proceedings of the previous night. "Now go right downstairs, please, and say that I am ravenously hungry, that I could eat my weight in eggs and toast, and that I want to take my breakfast upstairs in my room. Carry a nice full tray into young Ernie and then come back and see me. I have a plan."

"Oh, Miss, not a *plan*." It was as near to a wail as Carmine could get without actually wailing.

"Yes, indeed, and you are an important figure in it. Don't look like that, Carmine, I will not ask you to do anything difficult."

"That's what you said the last time," Carmine muttered.

"Yes, well, I miscalculated a little on that occasion but it all ended up just fine regardless. Anyway, this time you need only be ill."

"Ill?"

Rose, now standing, examined her maid with a critical eye. "Yes, ill. I think you look peaked. Much, much too pale. Doesn't your head throb?"

Carmine, at first ready to protest her good health, took one look at the calculating expression on Rose's face and gave up immediately.

"Yes, Miss, it does, throbs something fierce."

"I suspected as much. Your stomach doesn't feel very good, either, does it?"

"Not good at all."

"Excellent. Now go get our newest guest something to eat and don't forget to look a little pained whenever you get too close to the food."

"And who will help you dress?"

"I wouldn't need help if it weren't for that confounded corset, invention of the devil and scourge of womanhood. Have I mentioned I'm drawing the line at that ridiculous bustle contraption? Never mind, Carmine, I'm just chattering. You go and don't worry. I'll do the best I can and you can help with the last buttons when you get back, and don't forget you're ill."

"Something tells me it won't be that far from the truth by the time this is all over." But Carmine only said it under her breath and Rose ignored the grumble entirely.

Later, finally dressed, Rose stopped by the boys' room on her way downstairs. Ernie sat with the tray of empty dishes next to him and Piper was sitting up in bed, looking especially vulnerable with the bandage wrapped around his head. His cheeks, though, had more color in them than yesterday and he looked almost happy. She came in on the tail end of a story that made Piper chortle with delight. Just the sound of his laughter made Rose smile.

"That sounds promising. How do you feel?" She came up and laid a hand against his cool brow and saw no line of sweat beading along his forehead. Another good sign.

"I were hungry. Couldn't eat as much as I wanted, though. Stomach wouldn't let me." An even better sign, Rose thought.

"You said there was a doctor coming." This from Ernie in an accusatory tone that told her he still didn't trust her completely.

"There is but not for a while yet."

"I got to be going."

"Why?"

"Got things to do."

"Ah, I see." Rose looked Ernie over carefully. "Do you think you could put off your *things* for a little while and keep your brother company until the doctor arrives?"

He gave the interruption to his schedule serious thought and finally nodded.

"Good because I must make an appearance downstairs for a while." Rose gave the empty tray a look. "I see I don't need to ask if breakfast agreed with you. Will you promise to stay quiet and out of sight until I return?"

Ernie thought a little longer this time and nodded again.

"Very good. I'll trust your word on it."

Downstairs, Alice looked up as Rose entered the breakfast room.

"Well, you slept late again this morning, my dear. I'm afraid Forsythe already cleared the table."

"I'm not used to such rowdy evenings, Alice. It quite tired me out." Alice gave a snort at odds with her ladylike demeanor.

"Nothing tires you out, Rose, as everyone in the family knows. You have the same degree of energy your mother has always had and the same managing temperament. Not that I'm being critical," she added hastily. "You know I am excessively fond of Claire, but being in her general vicinity is always fatiguing and you are exactly like her."

"I'll take that as the compliment it was intended to be. Have you given any more thought to my belief that the excessive sentimentalizing of important issues such as we saw on stage last night does more harm than good to the cause of reform?" That question continued a discussion from the previous evening and occupied the two women until Forsythe entered the room and handed a card to Rose.

"I took the liberty of putting his grace, the Duke of Quill, in the front parlor, Lady Rose."

"Has his grace come to call on you again, Rose?" Something in Alice's tone sent a slight blush up Rose's cheeks. Rose felt the heat creep up her face and was both embarrassed and annoyed with herself but her expression did not reflect either of those emotions. Alice was amazed, having never seen the self-confident Rose blush before but she pretended not to notice. The whole exchange was very well bred.

"I mentioned to him last evening that Carmine was feeling unwell, and he kindly volunteered to stop in and take a look at her."

"I hope it's nothing serious."

"Stomach," Rose responded vaguely. "Head," adding with more truth, "I've no doubt she'll be fine."

"But Rose, why a duke to look at Carmine? I'm sure our own Dr. Billet would have done just as well."

"I meant no disrespect to Dr. Billet, but once his grace offered, I could hardly refuse without sounding either impolite or ungrateful."

"Yes, I can see that. So he does not plan to stay a while?"

"I can't imagine he will. He said he would stop by on his way to his surgery and I think it's just a pop-in. You needn't disturb yourself. I'll take him straight up to Carmine."

"But, of course, I must greet him, Rose. Whatever can you be thinking? It would hardly be proper for you to see him alone. In fact, I think I should take him upstairs to see Carmine. Now that I consider it, it would be even more improper for you to be alone with him there."

"I won't be alone," Rose pointed out. "Carmine will be there."

"Oh, of course." Alice still considered there was something not quite right about the arrangement, but when Rose explained it in her forthright way, she could not figure out what it was that felt wrong. Besides, Alice really did not want to take those extra steps to the guest wing because of the slight pain in her left knee, which made her think of lumbago and sent her into the front parlor to greet the doctor with an enthusiastic welcome followed by several lumbago-centered questions .

Rose enjoyed the ease with which his grace answered Alice's inquiries and said so on their way up the stairs. "You have been studying, your grace. My compliments."

"So you do not think I am making any of it up, then."

"You told me you didn't do so when it came to medicine."

"And you believed me? You don't strike me as a gullible woman, Lady Rose."

"I am eccentric but certainly not gullible. If you made that comment because I said I trusted you, please understand that I am very selective about those in whom I choose to place my trust."

"And I am on the list? I'm honored."

"As well you should be. It's a very short list."

Rose pushed open the door of the boys' room as she spoke and missed the quick, piercing look John gave her. He had thought she was making a joke and realized from her expression that she was not.

"You are a cynic, Lady Rose. I believe I'm shocked." She turned a surprised face to him.

"Oh, no, I'm not a cynic at all, only a discriminating realist. It suits me."

He would have responded to her comment but was arrested by the sight of two boys in the room instead of the anticipated one.

"What have we here?"

Ernie had risen at the opening of the door and now stood with legs akimbo and clenched hands at his sides, eyeing the two adults with suspicion.

Carmine, who had been sitting peacefully in a shadowy corner with a basket of mending at her feet, said sharply, "Now you mind your manners, young man. This here is his grace, Dr. Merton, the Duke of Quill, so let's not hear anything sassy." At that, Ernie gave the doctor a full look from head to toe.

"Go on. A duke can't be no doctor."

Rose sent Carmine a quelling look before saying to Ernie, "Of course, he can. There's no rule about it. This is Dr. Merton and he's come to be sure Piper is healing properly." To John she added, "This is Ernie, Piper's brother, who came for a visit last evening and stayed the night. I beg your pardon for forgetting to tell you about our latest addition to the household." John did not take his gaze from the older boy.

"A pleasure to meet you, Ernie. Now if you'll just step aside, I'll check out this young scamp."

Ernie did so, giving the doctor just enough room to get past but staying close enough in case he needed to spring to his brother's defense. Any doubts he had about the doctor's credentials disappeared as soon as John sat down next to the bed, however. The doctor spoke in a low, cheerful voice as he unwrapped the bandage around Piper's head, examined the already-healing scar, and then ran his hands along the boy's chest, arms, and legs. Rose, standing directly behind John, thought he had the most beautiful hands she'd ever seen, man or woman, although beautiful might not be exactly the right word for them. They were long-fingered, masculine hands but so firmly competent and gentle and expressive that just watching the exam engendered confidence. Apparently, Ernie felt the same for he relaxed and stepped farther away from the bed, although he continued to keep his gaze fixed on his brother. Finally, John sat back.

"You are a very fortunate young man, Piper, for it was a hard blow to a soft spot along your temple, but I see no reason why, with perhaps three more days of bed rest and another week without exertion, you shouldn't be right as rain. We want to give that hard head of yours time to heal completely inside and out."

"Excellent," said Rose. "You can stay here another ten days, and then we will discuss what happens next."

Piper, who had been quiet during the entire exam, finally spoke. "I can't stay here another ten days, can I, Ernie? Won't he find out and come after me?" Ernie's thin face took on a look of stubborn bluster.

"Never you mind about that. You do what the doctor says and I'll handle him."

"And who would that *him* be?" John asked with mild interest, but Ernie would not speak any more about it.

Instead, the older boy turned to Rose and asked, "How much to let my brother stay here like the doctor says?" Rose, too wise to protest that there was no charge, thought a minute.

"I'll make a bargain with you, Ernie. You be around if I need you to run errands and make deliveries and be willing to help cook out in the kitchen or Carmine if she asks and it will be a fair trade. We always have more work than help, don't we, Carmine?"

Carmine knew there was a lot of work to running a big house and could not dispute the foundation of Rose's offer, but she had her doubts about this scrawny, slightly-felonious child being of much assistance. She already felt she should lock everything of any worth carefully away in the safe.

"Is it a deal, then?" Rose persisted. "We could use your time and help more than your money."

Ernie thought through the ramifications of his acceptance. "I can only stay the mornings."

"That will do."

"All right, then."

Rose put out her hand and waited for the boy to put his own grubby hand with the skinned knuckles in hers. John thought she was the only woman of quality he knew who would make such a gesture and remembered how she had knelt in the street cradling Piper's head and later held his grimy form in her lap with his filthy hair and bloody face resting against her breast. It was all one in the same with Lady Rose Carlisle, the duke thought, and once more fleetingly found her entrancing. As soon as Ernie reached out his hand to shake Rose's, the feeling was gone, however, and it was back to the moment at hand.

"Got to go," Ernie said. He pulled a dirty cap over even dirtier hair and gave his brother a little punch on the shoulder. "You don't be no trouble now, hear? I'll be back sometime tonight."

"How will we know to let you in?" Rose asked. Ernie gave her a cocky grin in response.

"Weren't any need to let me in last night, were there? So you don't need to worry about it. I told you there ain't no place can keep me out if I wants to get in, even a fine house like this one." He slid out the door and by the time Carmine followed him and looked down the hallway, he had disappeared.

"I don't think we should allow that young man to roam the house at will, Miss."

"Carmine, I suspect your instincts are good and if there was something I thought I could do about it I would, but I have the feeling that young Ernie is exactly right and he will get in wherever and whenever he pleases. I for one do not intend to lose any sleep over it and neither should you. Piper, Carmine is going to be staying in here with you because she is unfortunately ill." The boy turned his dark eyes on Carmine and examined her without charity.

"She don't look ill to me."

"I know, but she is."

"I forgot to ask, Miss, what exactly is ailing me?" A meek but sensible question from Carmine.

"Stomach problems, I think, but no fever, since I don't want to alarm the rest of the house into fearing an outbreak of cholera. You need something from which you will recover in a few days. Maybe it should be nerves. What do you think, Doctor?"

"Anything," John replied, "except lumbago," causing a little gurgle of laughter from Rose.

"And I was just going to suggest a touch of the lumbago, besides. It seems a pity not to use it when we have one of the city's foremost experts on the ailment right here with us."

He met her laughing eyes with his and was conscious of an unexpected little start of pleasure at the sight. Lady Rose Carlisle might be eccentric, but she was also much too attractive for his own peace of mind. His grace had decided almost a decade ago that there was no place for a woman in his life, that there were precious few he held in any regard and that since he would always have to choose between a wife and his profession, it was the wife who must be banished. He was content with that decision and not about to see his firm resolve and years of bachelor routine disrupted. Those thoughts all ran through his mind quickly and left a residual frown on his face. Had Rose been any other woman, she would have been either offended or intimidated by his sudden stern look but since she was who she was, she gave his face a curious inspection and then turned away.

"Piper, you are to do exactly as Carmine says and Carmine, you are to look sick. Clutch your stomach and moan a bit if you should happen to see anyone. Thank you, Doctor. It was very good of you to come by. I've no doubt if you would like Ernie to run errands for you, as well, he'd be more than willing to do so." She turned and held open the door, smiling all the while, and followed him out of the room.

Walking together down the hallway, John replied, "That won't be necessary. I have more servants than one person needs or should be allowed to have. What do you know about Ernie?"

"Not nearly enough," Rose told him thoughtfully, "but earlier Piper mentioned someone called Rat Catcher. Does that name mean anything to you?"

When they reached the front door, Forsythe appeared with wraithlike subservience, holding John's hat and dampening their conversation.

John shook his head as answer, took his hat from Forsythe, and said cheerfully, "I think that with a day or two of rest, your Carmine should be back on her feet with no lingering effects whatsoever. I'll stop by again just to be certain and, of course, you can always contact me at my surgery. Good day, Lady Rose."

Rose had not even had time to sit down following his departure when Forsythe brought her another card.

"My goodness, I've become popular, Forsythe. Who is this now?"

It was the Baroness de Anselme, still dressed in mourning black but wearing a charming little bonnet that managed to look cheerful despite its somber color. When she saw Rose, the older woman's face lit up.

"You are home, Lady Rose. I am so pleased. I had hoped to be able to continue our acquaintance. Did I not just pass his grace, the Duke of Quill? It certainly looked like him getting into a carriage."

The two women went into the sitting room where Rose closed the doors before responding. "Yes, he came to check on our little patient at my request."

"Nothing wrong, I hope. I have thought of the boy frequently these last two days and lit several candles for him."

"His grace says Piper is healing nicely."

"Piper is his name? It suits him somehow, does it not?"

"He's certainly more of a Piper than an Ernie," Rose agreed and related the story of the older brother's nighttime appearance.

"So now there are two? Well, I do not think that changes anything on my part." Rose gave the Baroness a questioning look and the older woman went on to explain, "I came here today with a proposition, Lady Rose. My husband has—had—holdings on both sides of the Channel and after talking to my man of business, I find I have inherited a small country house and farm lands in Lancashire. I plan to visit there in the next few weeks and thought it might be just the place for the boy. Boys now, of course, but one more shouldn't make a difference. It is rural and I know these are town boys but if you thought it acceptable, I give you my word they would be properly cared for. They can help in the stables or the house, and there might even be some farmer's wife willing to care for them. I will not really know until I get there." She stopped speaking and waited hesitantly for Rose's reaction.

"Oh, Baroness, how very good of you! That would suit them exactly right and while it may take a bit of persuading, I think in the end they will be happy to go, especially once they meet you and you describe the glories of the country."

"But I do not know the glories of the country."

"Not the Lancashire country specifically, perhaps, but I feel quite confident that you will be able to describe the glories of some country somewhere in such a way that both Piper and Ernie will want to start out tomorrow. What a kind offer! I am much relieved, for truth to tell, I rather dreaded having to choose which of my long-suffering family was going to be the recipient of not one but two needy boys."

"You make a habit of rescuing children, then, Lady Rose?"

"Yes, I suppose I do, but I can truly say I have never left the house with that specific intention. Somehow it just happens, Baroness. I see something that troubles me and I cannot turn my back on it but must, as my father says, jump into the pond with both feet. He says he would feel much better if I would at least test the water with a toe before taking a plunge, and I do try to do what he says because he is the best father in the world and I would never purposefully distress him. Unfortunately, in times of high emotion I don't give a single thought to his advice. I'm afraid I am a very flawed daughter." But Rose twinkled when she said it, as if being flawed was not altogether undesirable.

"And still your father dares to leave you nearly unattended in the city in the care of only your pleasant but fluttering cousin. He cannot be so very worried about you then."

"He took Mother for a belated anniversary trip to the Continent and while I was invited to accompany them, I had no intention of intruding on their outing. I knew they wanted to spend time alone together and didn't need me along. I volunteered Cousin Alice's companionship and I could tell Father had his doubts, but he finally agreed. Fortunately, I am not a green girl fresh from the schoolroom and can get along in society without a great deal of fuss. Alice leads a quiet life without a lot of folderol and that suits me, so the arrangement is working out to everyone's advantage."

"You are not so very old whatever you may say, Lady Rose."

"No foot in the grave, it's true, but I am four and twenty with alas not a prospect in sight. I suppose I shall end up the family's spinster aunt, knitting mufflers in atrocious colors for all my nieces and nephews and descending on my siblings' homes at each holiday."

"If you are without prospects, it must be of your own choosing. You are a young woman of good family and some fortune, I would guess, well-spoken, warm-hearted, quite attractive, and possessed of the bluest eyes I have ever seen. Surely the men of England are not willfully passing you by."

"No, I suppose not, but those that cross my path seem so self-important and patronizing that I am sometimes impertinent, or so I have been told. I cannot tolerate being patronized, Baroness. It makes me so very cross that I find myself saying outrageous things in order to escape the conversation. Men of the present age are to a person offensively self-satisfied without an ounce of passion for anything but their own little lives. I cannot bear that." As she spoke, the mischievous good humor that had been on Rose's face was replaced by something else, something serious and almost scornful and, the Baroness thought, quite passionate in its own right.

"Yes," she said agreeably to Rose, "I can see that would not do for you at all. I cannot argue that there are a great many pompous men in the world, but I know from my own dear Pierre that all men are not so affected. Perhaps you relegate yourself to spinster aunthood prematurely."

Rose gave a wry little twist to her lips that belied her agreeable words. "You may be right, Baroness. Please forgive me if I sounded patronizing myself. My brother James is always chiding me about my lack of proper humility, but he's taking to the cloth so it is his duty to reprimand me, though I couldn't argue with him, regardless. He's absolutely right." Her serious mood dispelled, Rose moved the conversation on to safer ground.

When the Baroness rose to leave she said with a smile, "I met Lord and Lady Malarkey when they were in France last year, and they were kind enough to invite me to their spring soiree this Friday. It will be the first social event I have attended since my husband's death and I am intimidated at the prospect of facing a room full of strangers without him. How comforting it would be to know there might be more familiar faces there! I wondered if Lady Malarkey had extended an invitation to you and your cousin and if was too much to hope that you would both be in attendance."

"Alice mentioned the soiree, I believe, but truly, I don't recall how she responded. If it would please you, however, we will certainly attend."

Rose thought that behind the Baroness's smile a slight touch of anxiety shadowed her eyes and voice, and to promise attendance at an innocuous party seemed a small enough gesture of friendship. She liked the Baroness very much, was intrigued by the feeling of mystery about her, and touched by her air of vulnerability. If ever there was a woman of contradictions, it was the Baroness de Anselme, slight but with an impression of inner iron, self-confident but still shy, attractive and wealthy yet more careworn than her years seemed to warrant. The Baroness patted Rose's hand.

"How kind of you, Lady Rose! If there is any change in the boy's condition, do not hesitate to let me know." She drew her veil down over her face as Forsythe opened the front door for her but turned at the last moment to give Rose an appealingly diffident wave of her hand. Rose felt a little burst of affection for the woman and that was odd after only two meetings. What was even odder than affection was the feeling of familiarity she had for the Baroness, as if she had met her on a previous occasion or had known her for half a lifetime instead of half a week. There was something about the older woman that struck a chord in Rose's heart, friends from the start despite the differences in age and circumstance and nationality, none of which mattered between friends.

Ernie made a repeat appearance that night, sliding in through the bedroom door in such a stealthy way that he gave Carmine a start and even forced a quiet little gasp from Rose.

"Really," Carmine told him crossly, "you ought to at least knock. I'm getting too old for such surprises."

Rose, about to add with a wink that Carmine was a sick woman besides, never got the words out. She saw the bruise on the boy's left cheek, a splotch of deep purple streaked with shades of yellow that extended up under his eye.

Instead of her teasing remark, she went forward hastily, saying, "Why, whatever happened to you, Ernie? You look worse than your brother and he's the one we've been worried about." She reached a hand to touch his face but the boy jerked back away from her as if he thought she had been going to hit him. His sudden reflexive gesture made Rose narrow her eyes, seeing something in his frozen expression that made her suspicious.

"Did someone strike you?" she demanded.

Ernie shook his head, taking off his cap and going past Rose to Piper's bedside.

"No one laid a hand on me. I was in a hurry and run into a door. Like to knock myself silly and didn't it give me mates a good laugh?" He deliberately turned away from Rose so he faced his brother, and a wordless message that Rose was unable to catch passed between the two boys.

"Ernie's forever running into things. Ain't the first time he's had his eye blacked," Piper agreed. Ernie turned to look squarely at Rose and with Piper doing the same, she felt peculiarly on the spot, the two boys seeming to expect something from her and she at a loss as to what that something was. After a curious silence, she gave up on arguing the obvious.

"You should be more careful, Ernie. Someday you may do yourself serious damage and then who will watch out for Piper?" Turning to Carmine Rose said, "I'm going down to the kitchen, Carmine, to tell cook you feel better and could take some supper."

"I am that hungry, Miss, since I had to pretend to be off my feed all day."

"Yes, well, you'll need to figure out another way to get your nourishment because I won't be bringing supper up to you. It's for the boys. Don't look like that, Carmine. Neither of us is even close to withering away from starvation. I'll bring the tray up myself because everyone knows how devoted I am to you and will not find my doing so to be entirely ridiculous."

Rose said this with such an infectious grin that Carmine could not help but grin in return, but as Rose closed the door she heard the maid grumble, "All that devotion is like to be the death of me."

"She's a caution, that one," Ernie said to Carmine, nodding his head at the closed door.

"You mind your tongue, boy, when you talk about your betters." Then to take the sting out of the words, Carmine added, "She is a caution and I can't argue, but you won't find a young lady anywhere in town with half the heart and spirit of my Miss Rose."

Two days later Dr. Merton returned for an afternoon visit surprising Rose, who had just had Carmine pour hot water into a small tub for Piper and commanded him to take a bath and scrub himself top to bottom giving particular attention to ears and hair and feet and fingernails. He had not been amenable to the idea, stating with outrage that it "weren't Easter" and that was the only day his mum had ever made him take a bath. To which Rose had responded that if he did not immediately place himself in the tub, she would take the matter into her own hands and proceeded toward the bed with a look about her that said she was capable of doing exactly that without any qualms of conscience whatsoever. A small scuffle had ensued ending in giggles on both their parts, and she had turned her back as he took off the old, too-big bed gown he had been wearing and slipped into the water. Rose had then gone over to soap and rinse his hair and gotten splashed in the process. An accident, Piper said with a sly smile that made Rose laugh again.

"Accident my foot, young man, but I refuse to argue with a child and an invalid to boot. I've laid out fresh clothes for you so scrub yourself clean and then dry off and dress. I'll be back in a while and mind you, I will check those ears."

She had hurried down the stairs, small curls loose from her net and splashes of water still evident on her rumpled dress only to find Dr. Merton just stepping over the front threshold. Carmine, miraculously restored to good health, held open the door and gave a quiet groan of despair at Rose's appearance. Here she was, the daughter of a Marquis and the granddaughter of an Earl on her mother's side, and she looked like she should be taking in laundry.

For Rose's part, she knew Alice was resting and Forsythe was outside in the kitchen garden lecturing cook about the prominence of weeds among the herbs. That conversation, fueled by the antipathy of the two parties involved, was sure to continue for some time and Rose thought she could safely descend to the library without being seen. Piper did not know his letters, could not even write his name, and she was prepared to rectify that with the same ruthless determination that characterized all her efforts. All she needed was pen and paper and she was sure she'd have the boy writing his memoirs before he left for Lancashire.

John, perfectly well bred, pretended not to notice Rose's unkempt appearance but said pleasantly, "Good afternoon, Lady Rose. Forgive me for disturbing you, but I thought I would see how everyone is getting on in your household." He gave an amused glance at Carmine. "I am pleased to see that Carmine has made a speedy and total recovery."

Rose, whose dark brows had been drawn together in a look of thoughtful concentration, relaxed and responded easily, "The result of the happy combination of a naturally healthy constitution and good medical care. Now, please, do come into the front room. Carmine, hover around the door and step inside with us if you anticipate cousin Alice making an appearance. She will have my reputation in tatters if I am alone with a man, as if there were the slightest danger of inappropriate conduct with his grace."

For whatever reason, his grace found Rose's comment improbably insulting. His immediate reaction was to read into her words the hint that he was timid, inconsequential, and someone she didn't care a fig about and that even if he had the manly good sense to find a woman attractive it was the height of absurdity to imagine he would know how to act on the impulse. John surprised himself with such an unexpected but instinctive reaction, recognized it for the male pride it was and tried to banish the thoughts, but a little residual feeling caused him to lose the rather ingenuous and boyish smile that Rose had been admiring.

He had done that once before, Rose remembered, switched off his natural charm and surprising warmth and turned into a stern-faced man with a cool, almost disapproving expression. Rose, who had never in her life been intimidated by any man and was not about to start now, still found it a curious metamorphosis and felt a little pang of regret at the change. She smoothed her dress and tried to tuck her hair back into some order, then gave up, chuckling.

"No wonder Carmine gave me that despairing look. I was ensuring that Piper take a bath and somehow I got a bit disheveled in the process, but as a doctor I daresay you've seen your share of disheveled women so I won't apologize. Are you here to check up on our patient?"

John would have protested to anyone who had asked that that was indeed why he was there, but as an honest and introspective man he had realized at the first sight of Rose descending the stairs that Piper was only part of the reason he had stopped by the house on Pembroke Court. He found Lady Rose Carlisle so refreshingly intelligent, so sensible and candid with an endearing ability to laugh at herself—and, of course, there were those eyes—that he was drawn to her in spite of himself and all his firm resolutions. It was nothing he could say aloud, of course, so instead he answered her question with, "Yes. How is he?"

Rose filled him in on the younger brother's improvement, the Baroness de Anselme's Lancashire offer, and finally on the ugly bruise on Ernie's face, so black that it was just beginning to fade now, nearly three days later.

"And you got no more out of him?"

"No, but I'm sure someone struck him, only he's got such pride and such engaging valor that he won't admit it. I won't belabor it with him any more, though, because it won't do me any good and I believe both boys are willing to make the move to Lancashire. At least, I broached the subject and they didn't say no, and I don't want to say or do anything to ruin their cooperation. I'll tell the Baroness tomorrow night when I see her."

"How will you see her tomorrow night?"

"She mentioned that she was going to Lord Malarkey's soiree tomorrow evening and it would be the first time since her husband's death that she would be out in society, in a foreign country and among strangers making it all the worse. Since Alice and I were invited, I told her we would attend and lend her moral support. I like the Baroness very much, but I find her rather mysterious, don't you?"

"I can't say I consider her mysterious. In fact, there's something about her that makes one quite comfortable with her as if one has known her for ages. I think she is a shy and reclusive woman recovering from the grief of losing her husband, but I don't consider that to be mysterious."

Rose was unconvinced but said, "I agree that she is a comfortable and kind woman. Perhaps I have been reading too many gothic novels so that I must find mystery and suspense in everyone I meet."

"Surely not in me, Lady Rose." John didn't know why he made such a self-serving remark; he'd surprised himself and now felt faintly embarrassed.

Rose took the unexpected comment in stride, cocked her head and gave him a serious look before she opened the sitting room door and propelled him in her usual managing way into the hallway.

"Not mysterious exactly, your grace, but definitely a touch of the inexplicable." And with that cryptic sentence, she turned him over to Carmine, adding warmly, "I know you are a busy man so it was especially kind of you to take time from your day for us. I think Piper is well on his way to a complete recovery, and we will not need to trouble you again."

On his way home, John ran those words through his mind and found in them a dismissal of sorts, one that rankled. He was, after all, a peer of the realm and much sought after by unmarried young women and their matchmaking mamas, and here was a woman with water stains down the front of her dress calmly sending him away without a second thought. Then he laughed at his own vanity because he had scorned unmarried young women and their matchmaking mamas for the past several years and now preened about them as proof that he was still a sought after prize. What a pompous idiot he was! Coming into his own house, Rathbone met him at the door.

"Did I turn down an invitation to a gathering at Malarkey's tomorrow night, Rathbone?"

"Yes, your grace. You sent your regrets."

"Why didn't I want to go?"

"I believe your grace said something about deadly bores and off-key music."

"That was uncharitable of me. Please send a note around to them begging their pardon and saying that my plans have changed and I will be happy to attend, after all. Does Bellevue know what one wears to a soiree, do you think?"

"Yes, your grace. I'm quite sure he does and will be delighted to set out exactly the right apparel for the evening."

"I suppose you're right. He accuses me in his very correct way of being no challenge whatsoever for him." Then John went up the great staircase, whistling a melody he was making up on the spot.

A woman for sure, Rathbone thought, and God bless her.

Chapter 5

Rose, her cousin Alice, and the Baroness de Anselme converged on the Malarkeys' small ballroom almost simultaneously. The Baroness's eyes lit up when she saw them.

"I am so very pleased to see you. It is providential that we should meet so early in the evening." Her French accent was especially noticeable, Rose thought, and supposed that nervousness might make it so, since it had not seemed nearly as pronounced during their private conversations of the previous days.

"How lovely you look!" Rose told her, and it was true. The Baroness wore a long-sleeved dress of pewter gray a shade darker than her silver hair with her only ornamentation a striking brooch done in onyx and pearls lying at the base of the gown's high neck. Excitement or apprehension had colored her cheeks with a becoming pink flush and her brown eyes sparkled. Alice commented on the brooch and the Baroness's eyes sparkled even more, almost like tears.

"You are very kind to notice. My husband, Pierre, gave this to me many years ago and I wear it tonight hoping it will give me some of his confidence. He was a man of great good humor, a confident man who feared nothing, so perhaps it will help me past these foolish nerves. If he were here now, he would tuck my arm under his and say, 'Come, Juliana, life is passing us by. We have so much to do and so many people yet to meet. Come, come,' and we would go in together. And before the night was over every stranger in the room would be his friend."

"He sounds like a wonderful man," Rose said kindly.

"Yes, he was." The Baroness gave herself a little shake and straightened her shoulders. "He would be very, very disappointed that I stand here outside the party so let us enjoy the evening." She stepped through the door and turned to say to her two friends, "I will see you later in the evening, I am sure. Now I see Lady Malarkey and must greet her." The Baroness disappeared into a small crowd of people, Alice was snared by an acquaintance of her husband's, and Rose continued her way alone through the crowd toward the side of the room where several chairs were set up. She thought she would discreetly observe the Baroness just to be sure she was not isolated or cast adrift without a companion. It was not the type of evening Rose would have picked for herself. She enjoyed dancing a great deal, but the evening's orchestra played more for background music than anything else, which seemed to Rose to be a waste of perfectly good music.

Twice during her move across the room Rose was interrupted by young men who engaged her in conversation, asked her if she would like refreshments, and tried to convince her that she should sit with them. She recalled them vaguely from her first season and if it had mattered at all to her, she would have been chagrined that she did not remember any of their names. Fortunately it did not matter to her whatsoever so with her usual impeccable manners, she smiled, chatted politely, easily extricated herself from their company, and moved on, careful not to hurt anyone's feelings or be anything other than pleasant and unremarkable. Rose noticed the Baroness drifting toward the same grouping of chairs to which she was headed and would have happily joined her there except for the sudden figure of the Honourable Oswald Sweete-Cotton popping up in front of her like a child's spring toy. One moment Rose had a straight path to the far corner and the next a monocled and mustachioed face took up her entire line of vision. She considered herself ambushed and resented it.

"Lady Rose, I am very glad, so very glad to see you. I stopped by Pembroke Court one recent afternoon to see if you had recovered from that shocking affair with the horse and the boy but your maid said you were resting. Prostrate with shock, I shouldn't wonder, no, I shouldn't wonder at all. Wasn't the thing for a respectable woman to see, all that blood and the muck in the street, and it's perfectly understandable that you needed to rest after that. Must have been the most upsetting thing for a gently bred young woman like yourself. I tell you, we've got to do something about those young hooligans cluttering up our streets, causing hazards for decent folk. No respect for their betters is what it is, no respect at all." At this speech Rose, who had been feeling the tiniest bit guilty about so abruptly interrupting the conversation at their last meeting, lost any inclination to charity.

"The boy took a bad gash to the head and was nearly killed, Mr. Sweete-Cotton."

"Yes, well, tragic, I'm sure, but it ain't as if there aren't plenty of them to go around. One street boy more or less don't mean much to the rest of the world."

"About as much as the superfluous and inconsequential progeny of the upper classes, I should think," Rose responded tartly and turned away from him, thrown even more out of sorts by his puzzled look and furrowed brow, which told her he hadn't a clue about what she had just said.

She murmured the word *goose* under her breath in a tone of disgust only to hear someone behind her say, "I didn't see any *foie gras* at the refreshment table, but I am at your service if you would like to send me to look again." It was John Merton, looking especially handsome in formal dark tails, nothing pretentious or faddish about him, everything exactly right, even to the small white tie at his throat. Rose smiled to see him, smiled at his comment, too.

"Oh, dear, no one was supposed to hear that. I am not allowed to make unkind comments about anyone in a public setting. That was one of the first lessons I learned at my mother's knee and ordinarily I am scrupulous in following it. Some people make it very difficult to do so, however. Not that that's an acceptable excuse for bad behavior." Her eyes strayed to Sweete-Cotton standing where she had left him and apparently trying to figure out if he had been complimented or insulted. John's eyes followed her gaze.

"A friend of yours, Lady Rose? He looks confused about something."

"I daresay it is a perpetual state with him," she snapped, then gave a rueful laugh. "There, now I've done it again. Do not ask me any more about him or I shall be sunk beyond reproach."

He obliged, taking her by the elbow and steering her through the crowd to the corner where the Baroness sat lightly fanning herself and observing the assembly with a contented look on her face.

"I see our friend the Baroness has found a place outside of this press of people," John commented.

"Yes. I saw her earlier and was on my way to join her when I was intercepted. I think she is doing very well for a woman in a room full of strangers and in a country not her own."

They arrived to stand before the Baroness, John lifting the older woman's hand to his lips with just the right touch of courtliness. Her face was half hidden behind her ornate fan, but it was clear by the smile in her voice that his gesture pleased her.

"Your grace, how kind of you to take time from your evening to greet me! I saw you when you arrived but at the moment I was being introduced to a number of people whose names I have since forgotten and was unable to wish you good evening. Lady Malarkey said you sent regrets for the evening and I was surprised and pleased to see your familiar face among all these strangers."

"I thought I had a conflict, but when I found I was available after all, I could hardly wait to attend." Rose made a little choking sound next to him, but when he turned to look at her, she only raised her eyebrows and smiled a sweet smile. "I'm sure Lady Rose felt the same excited anticipation."

"Yes, indeed. Just last week I said to Alice that I longed for the opportunity to be crowded into a small room with inadequate ventilation, and if there was not the slightest chance for anything as enjoyable as a dance, my cup would absolutely overflow."

John could not help but laugh at her mischievous expression and the wry humor in her voice. She really was the most outrageous woman he had ever met, but despite her tart tongue, there was never anything mean-spirited or unkind about her. He found the way her blue eyes twinkled when she was saying something particularly shocking to be especially appealing. Since his first exposure to society, John had thought often enough that the world in which he lived was much like a large balloon that needed a pin prick to bring it back to ground, and he had tried to do so in his own way, with bland common sense and a certain reclusivity from the people and institutions that particularly irked him. Now, hearing Rose's playful comments and seeing her eyes alight with laughter, he decided he might abandon bland common sense for something more direct and humorous. Perhaps he took life too seriously. The thought had never occurred to him before.

The Baroness had laughed at Rose's comments, too, but added, "Lady Rose, I cannot help but think you would enjoy your evening more if you were not sequestered in the corner with me. I saw several young men watch you as you crossed the room, all hopeful admirers, I am sure. The color of your gown reminds me of fresh peaches and when the light catches you just right, it seems to glow. I recognize the fabric as *Satin Jean*, in Paris already last year but new to London, I think. I have not seen it on anyone else so I must compliment your progressive fashion sense. Does our friend not look charming this evening, your grace?"

John had thought the same since he had first seen Rose chatting with that insufferable coxcomb wearing the ridiculous monocle. At first sight he experienced the peculiar sensation that Lady Rose Carlisle was the only person in the room. All the noise had dimmed and everyone else had for the briefest of moments faded into the background. There had been only a young woman of medium height and delightfully feminine figure, her chestnut hair reflecting the light and dressed in a golden gown that showed lovely shoulders and a neck almost but not quite too long. Then the moment passed. Rose said something in a cool, dismissive tone—he could not make out the words—to her companion and firmly turned away from him, mumbling under her breath. John had spoken to her and she had turned the full force of those blue eyes, still fuming, on him, had recognized him, smiled with the barest chagrin, and it was almost as if that queer still moment had never occurred.

"Very charming." He answered the Baroness but looked at Rose with a warm smile that made the young woman's breath catch briefly in her throat. Turning to the Baroness, John added, "As do you, Baroness. You seem to be enjoying yourself. I hope the evening has not been too difficult for you."

"I expected that having to endure widow status would make me quite melancholy, but people have been kind and I find widowhood allows me more freedom than I expected. If I make some incredibly unfortunate faux pas, it reflects only on me and not on my dear Pierre. Bearing the responsibility for someone else's reputation can be quite burdensome." Her face sobered as she spoke and Rose thought she must be considering some serious circumstance from her previous life.

Rose began a response when from behind her came a clear, carrying woman's laugh, a high trill that was artificial and too loud and had the potential of becoming annoying in a very short time. She felt more than saw the duke stiffen beside her and looked up at him quickly. The smiling expression that had been there just a moment ago was gone, nothing soft or admiring in his eyes now. His face had frozen into a mask of polite indifference.

Rose turned toward the source of that distinct laugh and examined the woman with thoughtful care—short of stature, porcelain complected with artificial color staining her cheeks, ringlets of impossibly yellow hair cascading down onto bare, plump shoulders, full-bosomed, dressed in a gown of pastel yellow that was much too maidenly for her. Despite the cleverly applied color to her lips and the powder brushed on around her eyes, she was far too old for the ingénue role. The fair Penelope, Rose thought, and watched the woman approach their corner like a ship under full sail sending waves out around her as she navigated through the crowd, not to be diverted from her destination, which was obviously his grace, John Merton, the fifth Duke of Quill.

She stopped just behind John, placed a hand on his arm, and said, "Your grace." In a softer and more intimate tone she added, "John, it has been too long since I have seen you out and about. You have been a stranger. I trust you are well."

John turned toward her, gently and deliberately removed her hand from his arm, and answered, "Very well, Lady Fountain, and I trust the same for you and your family."

"Oh, yes, we are all well. I don't see my husband nearly enough because he is so busy at one or another of our estates, but I can't blame him. Our holdings are quite extensive, you know. He is here this evening, however, and I'll be sure to send him over to greet you."

Rose, catching a malicious undertone in the woman's words, took her into immediate, strong, and personal dislike.

"And how are your children?" his grace asked.

"Oh, a bother, as children must be, I suppose. We have left them in the country. Otherwise, how could we have enjoyed ourselves with them around?" Rose's initial dislike sprang into full-blown loathing. Despite the annoying trill of laughter that had followed her words as she attempted to turn them into an amusing joke, Rose thought the woman meant the remarks quite literally. Poor children.

After a brief, awkward silence, John said smoothly, "Have you met the Baroness de Anselme, Lady Fountain? And do you know Lady Rose Carlisle?"

The blonde woman murmured a pleasantry to the Baroness before she turned her sharp, dark eyes—so brown they were almost black—on Rose.

"I met Lady Rose two years ago."

"Indeed, Lady Fountain? Please forgive me, but I do not recall the meeting." Rose allowed only a touch of apology to color her tone.

"It was at Madame DuPree's, the milliner's, and it is quite understandable that you would not recall our meeting that day. You were incensed about some ragamuffin girl and were, as I recall, pointing your finger at Madame Dupree very forcefully while the little creature you defended hid behind your skirts."

Rose, seeing the speculative and rather spiteful look in the other woman's eyes, smiled. She had been right to dislike Lady Penelope Fountain and felt vindicated for her instinctive antipathy as soon as she spied the unkind gleam in the woman's eyes. For all her gracious manner as she related the story of the milliner it was evident to Rose that the woman did so with the intent to embarrass. A waste of her ladyship's time had she only known it because Rose had skin as thick as a walrus.

"Ah, yes, I recall the incident now and understand why I did not recollect meeting you. I was preoccupied with something important. How thoughtless of me! I hope you can forgive me." Rose smiled her sweetest smile, tilted her head just so, and raised her eyebrows to indicate she could not bear being unforgiven. Indeed, the look said, not having her ladyship's pardon would cast her into the doldrums for months, even years, to come. Only another woman would catch the slight, mocking edge to Rose's words and expression.

Lady Fountain missed nothing but answered with equal gentility, "Of course, my dear. Really, your defense of the child was quite touching." The tone of her words made it clear to Rose that she had found it incomprehensible and not touching, at all. "Now if you will excuse me, I must find my husband. He says he is quite helpless without me to steer him through this mass of people."

As she moved away, she placed her hand once more on John's arm and brought her cheek close enough to his to murmur in a low, suggestive voice meant for him alone, "Don't be a stranger, your grace. Surely you would have time to catch up with an old friend. His lordship is gone so often that I find myself quite bereft of company. Please plan a visit in the near future. I believe you must know where I stay in town."

If possible, John's figure became more rigid and for no reason Rose contemplated pulling the woman's yellow curls until she screeched. Her fierce moment disappeared along with Lady Fountain and his grace turned back to the two women with a little bow of farewell.

"Baroness, I wish you a good evening. You are safely placed into the hands of Lady Rose, who, I am confident, will keep you good company. Lady Rose, good evening."

His manner remained easy and pleasant but to Rose, who had come to know him surprisingly well in so short a time, he had lost the comfortable, good humor that had been there just a few minutes before. He seemed to go through the motions of civility while all the while wishing he were somewhere else, anywhere else but where he was at the moment. Rose had no doubt that he would be on his way home within the hour and the thought caused her a twinge of loss and regret. He was not yet gone and already she had lost interest in the party.

After John departed, Rose met the Baroness's eyes and for just a moment the two women thought as one.

"Would you like some lemonade, Baroness?" Rose finally asked.

"I believe I would prefer punch, Lady Rose. I find myself possessed of a sudden aversion for the color yellow." Rose accepted the comment as it was intended.

"I understand completely," she said and went in search of punch, the rosier the better.

As Rose had guessed, John did not stay much longer at the Malarkeys' soiree that evening, but she would have been surprised at the reason for his premature departure. She supposed that the sudden meeting with his former sweetheart had rekindled painful memories and that he might still have feelings for her. Even on short acquaintance, Rose knew the duke was a thoughtful man not given to quick or impulsive gestures, and for him to have been nearly affianced to a woman, no matter how impossibly pink and yellow she was, must have meant that his heart had been seriously and sincerely engaged. Rose, by nature compassionate and empathetic, felt inordinately protective of the doctor. Of course, he would leave, she thought to herself. It must have felt like a stick dragged against a wound to hear the woman one had loved—still did, perhaps, although one would think that after years of unrequited affection any such emotion would eventually fade away—talk about her husband and children in that gratingly smug way. Poor man. She hoped it had not been too painful for him. She may never have been a victim of passionate, unrequited love herself, but Rose could still appreciate how sensitive the situation must have been for him.

For his part, Dr. John Merton, the fifth Duke of Quill, was awash in conflicting emotions. Riding home, he sat inside the carriage and pondered the entire extraordinary evening. He had been startled to hear Penelope's laugh, had thought her to be still in the country and had not expected to see either her or his former friend Fountain in town, let alone at one of the few social occasions he decided to attend. John consciously tried to avoid Penelope, seeing her occasionally through the intervening years but only from a distance, not making eye contact and certainly not speaking with her at any length since their last meeting so many years before. For her to place her hand on his arm and use a tone that intimated continuing friendship had taken him aback, and he had felt an honest rush of emotion at the proximity. It was not at all the emotion he had expected, however.

That close, John had examined his former love with an objective eye, had noted the lines of discontent etched deeply around her mouth—now that he considered it, he believed their imprint had been there already years ago when he had first known her—had seen the brittle black of her eyes and wondered, he was a doctor after all, if so much plump, white flesh was really healthy for anyone. He had been surprised by the quick, sudden, entirely unexpected, and deeply felt pang of aversion he felt at her proximity and had experienced a hot embarrassment at her whispered invitation to renew their old friendship. How must that have sounded to Lady Rose with her candid gaze and the transparent honesty that was so much a part of her? Somehow Lady Rose's opinion of him had taken on great importance and he hoped she had not really grasped what Lady Fountain had been proposing. John, well aware of the underbelly of the society in which he lived, clearly heard the salacious invitation behind the woman's words.

For the past years the duke had considered there was but one woman he could love, and she had chosen to marry someone else. He had known a profound regret at the time and felt a sense of loss for the future he had planned—a home, a happy marriage, children, things he had not experienced from his own parents but which he knew existed because of his cousin Chloe and her doting husband, Charles, and because of Chloe's cousin Abby, very happily wed to the famous explorer William Penwarren. From the beginning he had hoped that he and Penelope would have just such a relationship, comfortable, supportive, and loving. When that had not happened, when Penelope had told him that she would marry him only if he gave up the vocation of medicine, which embarrassed her—"So beneath you, my dear. People will think you must work for a living out of necessity"—he had seen his vision of the years to come collapse. John, Duke of Quill, had grieved more than the loss of Penelope, had grieved the loss of the happy future he had anticipated as well. It had been a painful demise.

But tonight he felt none of that earlier distress. In fact, remembering how he had moped about after Penelope had told him about Fountain, how he had sequestered himself and thrown himself into his work at the expense of friends and a social life, how he had refused to be solaced but continued to nurse his grievance like some green boy, he could only shake his head. Whatever had he been thinking? This evening, seeing and hearing the woman he had once called *my Penelope* with fatuous devotion, John was conscious of only one overwhelming emotion and it was not love, regret, disappointment, jealousy, or sadness. It was relief, pure and simple.

Once home from the evening's inadequate revelry, Rose stopped by Piper's room expecting to see the two brothers asleep in the big bed that could have comfortably held at least another half dozen children. As late as it was, the boys were not asleep, however. A lamp still burned on the table by the bed where Piper reclined with his back against the headboard and Ernie sat upright on the small loveseat in the corner. Rose had the definite feeling that they waited for her. Next to Ernie was a third figure, smaller and pressed against him, asleep or close to it. Rose came in and quietly closed the door behind her.

"Who is this?" Rose asked, coming and crouching in front of the little figure that had toppled against the older boy in the unrestrained sleep of childhood.

"This is Evie."

"Ah, yes, Evie. And she would be—?"

"Our sis."

"Of course, I should have guessed."

Rose reached out a gentle hand and pushed back the little girl's tangled, dark hair for a better look. The child woke up and opened green eyes to study Rose. She couldn't have been more than four and had the same narrow, gamin face of her brothers, the same intelligent eyes with the same wary expression. It was an expression that hurt Rose every time she saw it.

"Hello, Evie. I'm sorry if I woke you."

The little girl straightened and reached out a hand with tentative intent to touch the sleeve of Rose's dress. She fingered it with wonder, then looked back up at Rose with wide and serious eyes.

"She thinks that's the prettiest dress she's ever seen," Ernie interpreted gruffly. "She ain't used to such finery."

Rose, who knew exactly how much the dress cost, was illogically ashamed. Sometimes the inequities of life were more than she could bear, although her father had told her a long time ago that it did no good to rue the facts. They were what they were and nothing could change them.

"It's how you handle the facts," her papa had told her, "and the attitude you take toward others that's important. Not that I understood all that until I met your mother, but she set me straight soon enough. If you sold everything and dressed in sackcloth, you'd still be the daughter of a Marquis with all the privilege and responsibility that comes along with the title. It can't be helped. Make the best of it, Rosie." Symonton called his daughter Rosie only when he was feeling particularly paternal and emotional so she knew he had been trying to get her to realize something important and profound. Time had helped her understand her father's words, but that did not mean she liked what she understood.

"Has she come to visit or to stay, Ernie?" Rose asked.

"I thought she could come to Lancashire with Piper and me. She's small and she don't eat much and she ain't any trouble. I'll be responsible for her. You won't even know she's here. She don't make any noise since she stopped talking."

"Stopped talking? Doesn't she speak at all?"

"Not since Mum died. She ain't said a word in over a year."

"Oh." Rose invested the word with soft sympathy. "Of course, she can stay and I'll talk to the Baroness tomorrow. I can't imagine there's not enough room in Lancashire for one little girl. Are there other brothers and sisters you intend to spring on me? Because if there are, please do them all at once and not one at a time. My nerves aren't up to it."

"This is all there is," Piper said from the bed. "There's just the three of us." Rose, standing and seeing the three little figures that sat stiffly in the shadowy room, unaccountably felt tears prick at the back of her eyes, which caused her to speak more brusquely than usual.

"However many there are of you, you would all be welcome, but I admit that I'm glad we're stopping at three. Stowing away more than that would be a difficult task, even for me. Now crawl into bed and go to sleep. I'll see you in the morning and figure out some way to have breakfast sent up for you."

"Like as not, being out late made you powerfully hungry." This from Ernie, who had adjusted readily to Rose's style.

Rose laughed at that. "Like as not," she agreed.

"Well, you don't have to find nothing for me," he went on. "I'll be off early before anyone in the house is up. You'll watch out for our Evie, then?"

He stood, pulling the little girl up with him, oddly defiant and yet so vulnerable that Rose felt a lump in her throat. What a level of trust he offered her! She was humbled beyond measure.

"Indeed, I will. I promise, but it's late now and we should all be sleeping. Blow out the lamp and crawl in. We'll talk tomorrow." With the lightest gesture, Rose flicked a finger against Ernie's cheek. "You're a good brother, Ernie. Your mum would be proud."

He blinked at that and almost smiled, caught himself before the smile escaped, and said with forced gruffness, "Well, don't be getting the wrong idea. I ain't soft."

"No, indeed. Not soft at all," Rose agreed and went on to her own room. She supposed she would have to do something about the situation. She couldn't have the entire north wing filled with street children. Eventually all the house servants would know, if they didn't already, and Forsythe would find out and go in outrage to Alice, who would worry about what her husband would think and distress herself about the situation until she made herself ill. Then she would come hesitantly and apologetically to Rose to tell her the children must go. The whole scene played out in Rose's mind as a Delphic vision of the future.

Carmine waited for Rose in her room to help her undress, and from her casual words it didn't appear the maid was aware of the newest addition to the Pembroke Orphanage.

"So how was your evening, Miss?"

She unfastened the buttons down the back of Rose's dress and unlaced the corset. Not, thought Carmine, that her young lady needed a corset with that little waist of hers, just one part of her pretty figure and lovely posture and the right amount of curves. A pity Rose did not spend more time enhancing those particular attributes, but she had always been a girl without a lot of patience for fripperies. Not much vanity there but plenty of spirit, which served just as well.

"Very interesting, Carmine." Carmine was used to Rose chattering on about the people with whom she had spent the evening—not always charitable chatter, either—and was surprised at how quiet her young lady seemed this night.

"Was the Baroness there and his grace, too?"

"Yes to both." Rose crawled between the covers. "You go to bed, Carmine. I'm sorry you had to wait up for me." Carmine looked at her in astonishment.

"That's my job, Miss. I always see you to bed."

"Yes, I know, as if I am a child, as if my needs are more important than your comfort." The tousled, mute, green-eyed little girl down the hall had left an impression on Rose that would not go away. She looked up, saw Carmine's puzzled look, and smiled ruefully. "Ignore me. I have had to endure an evening in a stifling room crammed full of people I didn't know, and on top of all that Mr. Sweete-Cotton was there."

"I do hope you minded your manners, Miss," Carmine's tone suitable for a small child prone to willful and undisciplined outbreaks of temper. Rose was not offended.

"Of course, I did, but it was difficult. He really is such a dunderhead, you know."

"Yes, Miss, I daresay you're right, but didn't his grace's presence help make the evening a little more pleasant?"

An expression flitted across Rose's face, something so transitory that only Carmine with her years of experience could distinguish. It was an odd, soft look and seeing it, Carmine felt a suspicion that made her heart flutter. Could it be that her young lady was at long last interested in a gentleman? The maid had never thought to see the day and went to her adjoining room rejoicing. The only thing more fitting for her young miss than being a duchess was being the queen, but since that title was already taken, duchess would serve just as well.

Chapter 6

When Rose peeked into the children's room in the morning, Ernie was already gone, Piper was up and dressed, and Evie was sitting cross-legged in the middle of the bed. She had on her little face a beatific expression, as if the comfort of a featherbed was completely new to her. Very likely it was, thought Rose.

Carmine was already there, hands on hips, speechless and staring. She turned at Rose's entrance.

"Well, I never, Miss. Here's another one. Whatever will we do?"

"I am assured this is the last of the stowaways and I think we should get hot water so I can give Evie a good wash. Have we anything small enough for her that she could put on afterward?"

"Evie, is it?"

Carmine, about to ask Rose how she knew the little girl's name, gave up on the question before she ever voiced it. What did it matter, anyway? Apparently, they were going to continue to add children to the north wing until the creatures hung out the windows and slept on the roof, and she might as well accept the inevitable. She had protested the milliner's little girl every step of the way, but Rose had ignored her with blithe indifference and readied that child for her new home in Sussex where she continued to live a happy life as the well-fed ward of old Feastwell, Rose's grandfather's cook at Loden Hall. Carmine had learned the futility of protest during that escapade and never again objected with the same vociferous fervor. If Lady Rose felt she had to do the right thing, she would do it and the rest of the world, above or below stairs, could be hanged. Carmine prepared to deliver hot water and a substantial breakfast.

"Tell cook," said Rose with a wink to Piper, "that being out late last night made me powerfully hungry."

Carmine could have told her that cook and most of the downstairs staff had already figured out that something was amiss in the north wing. The house servants' universal dislike for Forsythe bonded them together in a conspiracy of tolerance that would have allowed Carmine to drag an entire milk cow up to the second floor if she so chose without one raised eyebrow from anyone. The staff also felt a certain pride in Lady Rose's good nature and amusing eccentricity, always such a pleasant young lady without being too familiar and never top lofty. They were invariably cheered when they heard she was coming for a visit, which was not nearly often enough in their collective opinion. A visit from Lady Rose promised several weeks of light-hearted relief from the otherwise unmitigated dullness of the Farmington household. Thus, for all they cared Rose could have harbored a troupe of traveling gypsies upstairs. The pleasure of keeping it from Forsythe only heightened the enjoyment.

Later, Evie, glowing from the scrubbing Rose had bestowed and dressed in makeshift clothes much too large for her, sat on Rose's lap and allowed her hostess to brush through the child's thick, knotted hair. Once or twice Evie winced when Rose caught a snarl and Rose hastily apologized, keeping up a monolog of stories and chatter as she finished the chore. When she finished, she pulled the girl's hair back with a ribbon.

At the sight of it Piper, who had been watching the enterprise, said, "See, Evie, I told you I'd find you a ribbon. It ain't red, mind you, but that green is just as nice," and Rose had a sudden memory of a red ribbon dropping from the boy's hand into the dirty street looking like just another stream of blood. She thought she would never take such a pretty trifle for granted ever again.

When Ernie reappeared in the afternoon, Rose sent him with notes to the Baroness and the Duke of Quill. She explained the situation to both of them, asking one if she thought there would be room for a third child—a very small and quiet third child—on her Lancashire estate and asking the other to stop by, however briefly, to examine the newest addition to the family.

The note waited for John when he returned home in the afternoon and he promptly put his hat back on, saying to Rathbone, "I have been summoned, Rathbone. Apologize to the kitchen for me, since I will miss tea. Was there any other mail of which I should be aware?"

"There is an invitation from your cousin Chloe, your grace."

John's cousin Chloe, her husband and young daughter, and her brother Augustus now at university were the duke's only family. He trusted them explicitly and without hesitation, felt unqualified comfort in their presence, and loved them without reservation. The invitation was to a dance Chloe and her husband were hosting.

"Please come, John," Chloe wrote in her own hand. "You have played the hermit too long. I promise you will enjoy yourself." Putting the invitation back into its gilt-edged envelope, he considered the idea of a dance with surprising good humor and even some anticipation. Perhaps Lady Rose would be there. Chloe's husband and Farmington were political colleagues—well, more like political adversaries but *cordial* adversaries—and it seemed likely that Alice might be asked to attend along with her visiting cousin, Rose. John didn't give much thought as to why the idea was so cheering, only that it was and he would have to remember to ask Rose if she planned to attend.

Rose, who knew nothing about the party and hadn't the slightest idea if Alice had been invited to such a dance, answered John's polite question with assurance.

"Why, yes, I'm sure if it's a political associate of Mayhew's Alice will want to go, and since your cousins are hosting, the guests will certainly be a cut above the Malarkeys' crowd. I am not allowed to disparage and I don't mean to sound superior, but I must say that some of the people there that evening were a disappointment. Didn't you think so?" She looked at John with her wide, guileless, blue eyes and he found himself thinking of Penelope and agreeing, although he knew he ought to be more properly noncommittal.

"Now tell me about your latest addition," he requested.

Rose did so finishing up with, "I wish you would look at her little hands and fingers. They seem to be too calloused and cramped for such a young child. I think it might be from needlework, from holding the needle for long periods of time and pricking the tips of her fingers instead of a thimble. She does not speak, either, and I thought you could assure me that there is no physical reason for that condition. She seems well, otherwise, but too thin and I will feel better knowing you have given her a thorough examination."

John thought that Rose looked particularly attractive that afternoon, her cheeks flushed with the same color as her name and her eyes bright. It appeared that the previous late night had had no ill effects on her and he told her so.

"Alice and I did not stay much later than you, your grace. Once I was assured that the Baroness was comfortable and at ease, making new acquaintances and enjoying herself, I had no need to stay. There was music but it was not intended for dancing, and since that is the only social pastime I truly enjoy, I had neither the desire nor the need to remain any longer than was absolutely necessary."

"Since you enjoy dancing, will you reserve a dance for me at my cousin's party, Lady Rose?"

The unexpected request startled him almost as much as it did Rose. She had been having a perfectly proper conversation with his grace, Carmine knitting unobtrusively in the corner to obey the proprieties, and suddenly his voice had changed from light-hearted banter to something more serious. It caused her gaze to fly to his face and examine the expression there.

After a tiny pause, she said pleasantly and with no hint in her voice of the sudden breathless feeling she had experienced at the look in his eyes, "Of course. I would be delighted, but I warn you that I have been told by less worthy partners that I sometimes usurp the lead." The remark made him smile and the brief, awkward moment passed.

"I can't imagine why that does not surprise me, but I will take the risk. Now how have you planned for me to see your young patient without arousing suspicion?"

"Carmine is going to injure her ankle." In the corner where she sat, Carmine raised her head in the manner of a forest animal sensing danger.

"Like Philip's daughters, have you received the gift of prophecy?"

"You needn't sound so skeptical, your grace. Carmine is going to trip at the top of the stairs as I bid you farewell and you are going to sprint to her rescue."

"Sprint? Would it not be just as effective if I merely hurried?"

"No, no," answered Rose, laughing at his tone, "I have my heart set on a sprint."

"But sprint *up* the stairs? I'll be quite winded."

"You will be fine. You look to be in very good shape and I'm sure you are well able to sprint up any number of stairs."

She followed her observation with a faint but becoming blush, which John noted but did not understand. Along with her comment, Rose had the thought that the doctor really was in very good shape, nice broad shoulders with no need for padding, muscled legs and a trim waist that bespoke regular exercise and perhaps even time in the boxing ring. For whatever reason, she was suddenly very aware of him as a strong and attractive man and the thought flustered her, an entirely new and confusing feeling.

Fortunately, Carmine interrupted to ask in a voice made stoic by experience, "Shall I twist my ankle and fall, Miss, or just give out a little yelp?"

"Oh, I don't think you need to fall, Carmine. We may ask his grace to sprint up the stairs to your rescue, but I fear that asking him to carry you to your room would be too much of an imposition. Not," she turned to John with an innocent look, "that I think you couldn't carry Carmine to her room, but I don't want to take advantage of your good nature any more than is necessary."

"Your thoughtfulness is exceeded only by your creativity," he murmured in return and was rewarded by one of Rose's bright smiles.

"What a good sport you are!" was all she said but for just a moment he felt she had handed him the moon.

The plan, as all of Rose's plans usually did, worked perfectly. Carmine had started up the broad staircase as Rose bade good-bye to the doctor under Forsythe's watchful eye when there was a sudden cry from the top of the stairs. John sprinted—Rose thought she had been exactly right; he was in very good shape and not winded a bit by the ascending rush—to Carmine's side with Rose on his heels. Forsythe, caught with the Duke's coat and hat in hand, could only stand at the foot of the steps, looking up, trying to see what was happening through the flurry of activity.

"Oh, dear, Carmine, what have you done?"

"I don't know, Miss," Carmine answered honestly. "I took the top step and my foot just twisted under me without warning."

"Would your grace mind helping her to a chair?"

"Not at all." John was smooth, too. "And I should take a look at that ankle to see if it is beginning to swell."

"We'll be down in a moment, Forsythe. Please wait there with his grace's hat until he returns." That would keep Forsythe in his place, Rose thought, following Carmine and the doctor into the room where the children waited. She closed the door behind them.

It was clear that Evie took to John from the start. She sat with tolerant patience as he looked her over carefully, examined her hands, wrists, scrawny legs, and scabbed knees, looked in her mouth, felt her throat and neck, carefully tapped her concave little chest, and finally ran a feather-light hand over the back of her head. Then he sat back on the chair, both hands on his knees, and smiled at the child that sat across from him on the edge of the big bed with her eyes wide and fixed on his face.

Will you talk to me, Evie?" he asked. "I know you could if you wanted to. There's nothing to keep you from speaking." He waited for a response until she finally gave a small shake of her head, still not taking her eyes from his face. "Well, then, that's fine. I expect you'll decide when the time is right and surprise us all by bursting into song." Which to everyone's astonishment, including Rose's, the doctor proceeded to do himself, finishing off a muted but boisterous chorus of a particularly silly ditty about mermaids and sailors.

"I'm a sailor man on the ocean blue /
And I've seen wondrous things a time or two /
But the queerest sight to turn me pale /
Was the vision of a woman with a long, green tail. /

O, fish and fin and gill and scale, /
'Twas the vision of a woman with a long green tail."

He sang in a rich, true baritone, prolonging the word *scale* on a high and dramatic note that made everyone at first stare and then break into spontaneous albeit carefully quiet applause.

"That," declared Rose recovering from her surprise and the lurch her heart gave at the man's unexpected playful kindness to the little girl, "was really splendid. You see, Evie, what you miss by not speaking? You and Dr. Merton could take to the stage in a song and dance revue. I can picture it in my mind now." The little girl opened her mouth and gave a whisper of a giggle.

Progress, thought John with satisfaction, which was his intention all along.

Later, Carmine directed to stay behind and reminded not to forget to limp for a day or two, Rose saw John down the stairs. He had told her that while undernourished, there didn't seem to be anything wrong with Evie that good food and safe surroundings wouldn't cure, concluding with, "I don't know about her voice, though. I couldn't find a physical reason for her not to speak and I can only assume the reluctance is in her mind. Unfortunately, we don't know much about the brain but I've read of similar cases. Some doctors call it a type of hysteria, where a strong emotion has paralyzed one or another of the senses."

"Can she recover?"

"Some do. It's hard to tell, but I think she stands a good chance of doing so. Evie is very young and with you watching out for her, she will know she's secure and cared for and she may be able to relax whatever emotion it is that keeps her mute."

They reached the front door where Forsythe reappeared with John's hat and coat, saying, "No lasting damage, I trust, Lady Rose," his small eyes alive with a suspicion that belied his bland tone.

"Oh, no. We are fortunate that Carmine will be back to her normal self by morning, but his grace has suggested she stay off her feet until then."

"That one's had an unfortunate run of bad luck and ill health of late." The butler's tone was still nondescript but Rose was no fool.

"Carmine, you mean? Yes, now that you mention it, she has, and they say things run in threes so I tremble to anticipate what tomorrow will bring." Rose appeared to contemplate all sorts of calamities with good cheer. "It is so providential that the duke has been handy throughout and I refuse to worry about the future."

John slipped into the coat Forsythe held, saying as he did so, "Very wise. I can't imagine there is anything to worry about, and I offer my professional opinion that by tomorrow Carmine will be healed and back to her usual sure-footed self."

"Like Philip's daughters, have you received the gift of prophecy this time, your grace?" asked Rose, straight-faced.

John met her mischievous look with an appreciative and amused one of his own before answering, "Apparently. Who would have thought it a contagious condition?" He descended the front steps toward his carriage with a sprint similar to his recent ascent.

After he left, Rose sought out her cousin Alice, who had been out most of the afternoon and had settled into the library to go over menus and account books. She looked up when Rose entered.

"Did I hear company?"

"The Duke of Quill stopped by to confirm Carmine's full recovery."

"Indeed? He has been quite thoughtful in that regard."

Alice said no more but there was something in her tone that caused Rose to say hurriedly, "Yes, well, he did say it was directly on his way home from his surgery and he only stopped a moment." As if she were in a hurry to change the subject, Rose asked, "Cousin, have we been invited to an evening at Chloe Fitzhugh's?"

"How did you ever know that? I've only recently had the invitation."

"Oh, there's word about town," said Rose, her tone hinting that she had troupes of town friends rushing to her front door to share such information.

"Does it interest you?" Alice, who was used to having to beg Rose to attend any social event, waited for the answer with interest.

"I thought it sounded agreeable. There will be dancing, you know, and I love to dance. I've never met Chloe Fitzhugh, but you've spoken highly of her more than once, and I've heard she's very talented and very pleasant, and I think I should like to meet her."

"She is indeed very talented on the keyboard and the harp, especially, and she is very pleasant, as well. A nicely-bred young woman with good manners and a lively disposition, much like you now that I think of it, but a few years older. Did you know she is the Duke of Quill's cousin?"

"I may have heard something to that effect. I really can't recall." Rose did not meet her cousin's eyes. "So may we go? I think it will be a good antidote to my evening with the Malarkeys and yours with the Bennetts."

"Of course, Rose, if you would like to attend, I will send word that we will be there. Perhaps you should get a new gown for the occasion." Rose, recalling Evie's pinched face, shook her head.

"That would be an unnecessary extravagance. I brought several gowns with me, and they will be new to a town audience because I have not worn them since my arrival. I'm sure I can find something acceptable."

"Blue," said Alice.

"I beg your pardon."

"I said blue. I think you should wear something blue. It's so attractive with your eyes and your skin and when you are dancing you get the most becoming color in your cheeks. It would be perfect. I can picture the evening and I see you in blue."

"I don't recall that you've had these streaks of imagination before," laughed Rose and went immediately to her rooms to explore her closets, looking for exactly the right gown, something the color of the sky on a summer day, the color of gentian and cornflowers and delphiniums. Alice was not the only one with a vision.

After two more days, Piper was up and about and restless in the confines of his room regardless of its huge size. Rose, in the cheerfully persuasive way she had, coaxed him into learning his letters and found him to be a quick and intelligent pupil. The still silent Evie listened to the lessons as she played in the corner with an old doll and doll bed Rose had pulled out of the attic, something that had once belonged to Alice's daughter, who was now a wife and mother herself. The toy was old but from Evie's expression almost too fine to be handled. Evie would stop playing and come over to lean against Rose's knee and listen whenever Rose read a story aloud, watching with her wide, inquisitive eyes as Rose pointed at the words she read. The process of letters and words on the page coming alive into sounds and stories seemed to fascinate the little girl.

The night before the Fitzhugh party, Rose woke in the night and could not get back to sleep regardless of the tricks she used to induce slumber. Sheep jumping over stiles did not help, and she twice made it through the books of the Bible in reverse order and still lay awake. She was conscious of an unusual excitement but could not have said exactly what prompted her happy anticipation. Rose had been to other parties before and danced at other dances, more, in fact, than she cared to remember. Her parents had allowed her first formal season in society at twenty, older than most of the other girls but the Marquis of Symonton, despite his dissolute bachelor reputation, had to many people's surprise become an old-fashioned and protective husband and father. He felt no rush to marry off his youngest child, which was fortunate because she had not been married off that season or the next, and Rose herself had finally made the gentle suggestion that perhaps she had used up all her seasons. At four and twenty she believed there was no social activity she could contemplate with anything other than desperation or dread. Rose found all the superfluous chatter, the insincere flirting, the extravagance, and the entitlement numbing to the extreme, but here she lay, picturing the blue gown she would wear, considering how she would fix her hair and how exactly right the aquamarines at her ears and throat would look. She was as wide awake as if it were noon and not well past midnight.

Throwing on her wrap, she decided to pad down to the kitchen for a piece of cook's tea bread, which suddenly took on the same appeal as the Eden fruit to Eve. The house was very quiet, and, careful not to make a noise that would roust Carmine from her slumber, Rose pulled her door shut quietly with both hands and turned back into the dimly lit hall. Farther down the hallway she spied a figure.

At first she could not believe it was a figure at all, thought it must certainly be a shadow or a trick of the flickering wall sconces. But, no, it was a man, dark and ominous even at a distance. He seemed to be concentrating on the door and reaching for the handle of the children's room. With the collar of his heavy coat turned up he looked headless in the gloom, like the horrible figure in *The Legend of Sleepy Hollow* she had read years ago, forced to hide the pirated book of stories in the stable and read it in secret because she knew her mother would have thought her too young for the story and not allowed it.

Rose was grown up now, though, and did not believe in headless, haunting figures. Without conscious thought and with no fear whatsoever she went quickly forward.

"Here," she said clearly, "who are you and what are you doing? Get away from there." Her voice carried in the still hallway and the man raised his head and turned toward her to reveal a vicious, stubbled face with a wispy, whiskery moustache that, combined with his narrow, sharp nose, made him resemble a particularly nasty rodent. Intuitively Rose knew who it was.

"You, Rat Catcher, get away from that door," she said, fury and outrage coloring the words.

"So you know who I am, do you?" He had a sibilant voice that stretched out the s sound in a nasty, hissing way. He turned toward Rose but made no move away from the door.

"You, sir, are a villain and now you are a housebreaker. I will have you arrested." He ignored her words.

"You has my property, lady, and I wants 'em back."

"Children are not property. Now get out. I will scream the house down and call the authorities immediately if I see you again." Rose stood her ground, eyes blazing. Behind her, Carmine's door opened and the maid stepped out into the hallway.

"Miss, what is it?"

The scoundrel took a quick look at Carmine approaching and knew he hadn't much time.

"I'll have my goods back, lady, so you'd best watch your step and theirs, too." He pivoted quickly and disappeared down the shadowy hallway and through the same servants' doorway Rose and the doctor had once used to carry an unconscious Piper to his room.

Carmine came up behind her to say with quiet fear, "Oh, Miss, who was that and how did he get in?"

"That," Rose replied grimly, "was as nasty a piece of work as I have ever seen, and I imagine he got in the same way Ernie gets in. Don't say anything to anyone about this, Carmine."

"But, Miss, we can't have half of London parading through the house while we sleep. It fair makes me shiver just thinking about it."

"I couldn't agree more but don't worry any more tonight. He won't be back. For all he knows we're sending for the authorities right now. I'll talk to Forsythe in the morning about increasing security."

"What about the children?"

"The children will be fine," Rose replied with forbidding gravity. "I should like to see anyone get past me to do them harm. Now go back to bed. The adventure's over." But later, curled up in the loveseat in the children's room, periodically dozing and watching Piper and Evie sleep, Rose knew the adventure was not over at all.

In the early morning, she went back to her own bed and slept easily, then awakened refreshed and energetic. She was not a young woman to carry the night's hobgoblins into the light of day. Instead, in a matter-of-fact, thoughtful tone she shared her meeting with Rat Catcher of the night before with the newly-arrived Ernie, watching an unchildlike expression of fear and loathing cross his face. No one, she thought, child or adult should look like that at the sound of another person's name, and she resolved even more to send all three of her young charges off to a happier, safer life. Rose wrote a hasty note to the Baroness and sent it via Ernie, bidding him wait upstairs with his siblings when he returned. She herself dressed to go out.

"But, Miss," Carmine told her, "you have the party this evening and you don't need to be gallivanting about. We should decide on your hair and your gown and your shoes and what you'll wear at your throat."

"I have that all taken care of." Rose pulled on gloves and readied herself to descend the staircase to the front door. "The sapphire combs, blue, patent dancing slippers, and aquamarines so you see there's no need to fuss." With that she was out the door and into the waiting carriage.

Chapter 7

The Baroness had moved from the Savoy to a town home in a modern, quietly elegant neighborhood, a place discovered by respectable families with new money and like the people who lived there was well kept and carefully groomed. The area was new to Rose, who appreciated the graceful front windows and small beds of flowers along the walks.

"There's even a park at the end of the street," the Baroness told Rose as they sat in the elegant front parlor. "It is quite lovely with ducks and a pond. There are not a lot of children in this neighborhood, I am sorry to say, but there are a few and they seem to enjoy all the greenery." The remark was a fitting segue for Rose.

"I was hoping we could add three more children to the neighborhood," she began and went on to tell her friend of the alarming confrontation in the hallway the night before.

"But, Lady Rose, surely you contacted the authorities after such a startling and it seems to me dangerous meeting."

Rose shook her head. "No, how could I without giving the game away? I talked to Forsythe about believing I'd seen someone disreputable skulking about the rear of the house and asked him to be sure the house was firmly secured each night but to mention anything about the children would only cause a great hubbub. Forsythe would gloat, Alice would become upset all out of proportion to the circumstance, and everyone in the house would be thrown into a tizzy. The inevitable result didn't seem worth the effort, not if you were willing to take the children. I thought of asking Dr. Merton because I understand he rattles around in some monstrously large house, but he is gone all day and what would Piper and Evie do all by themselves? Besides, Evie needs a woman's touch, I think, poor thing. She is just now unfurling like a flower that's been kept in the dark and has finally been exposed to light. I would hate to have her curl up inside again."

"But she has not spoken yet?"

"No, not a word, but I truly think she will. She is a little pitcher with big ears, doesn't miss a thing, smiles at my jokes such as they are, and just yesterday she crawled into my lap of her own accord. I don't know how long you plan to remain in town, but to me it made sense to move the children in with you now since you will be taking them to Lancashire eventually. I understand their presence may at first seem inconvenient, but it is for a short while and they are very, very quiet children. I daresay you will not even notice they're here." The Baroness sat back with her eyes fixed steadily on Rose's face. Then she gave a sigh followed by a quick smile.

"You are a remarkable young woman, Lady Rose. I cannot imagine there is anyone else that could persuade me not only to volunteer to move three unknown street children to my country home, but even to take them into my town home. It is exactly the kind of thing Pierre would have loved. He was enamored of children."

"Do you have children of your own, Baroness?" Rose could not recall that the woman had mentioned anything about progeny during any of their conversations and surely if there were offspring, the older woman would not be traveling on her own to handle her husband's business affairs. Still, it did not hurt to ask.

"We were not blessed with them, I am afraid. It was a grief to us," and added in a soft tone, "I lost a son."

"I'm so very sorry. I can tell it was a grief. How senseless life is sometimes! You would have made a wonderful mother." At that the Baroness turned her glance away.

"I wonder," was all she said but there was a tone to her voice that struck Rose as terribly sad and full of regret. The Baroness stood quickly, hiding her grief behind a brisk and business-like tone. "Go and fetch your children. I will let Giselle know to expect them and have rooms made up. They will be happy here and safe, I hope. We will be off to

Lancashire by the end of the month so it is only a short stay for all of us." She took Rose's arm to walk her to the front door when she stopped suddenly to rest her palm against the younger woman's cheek. "I am proud to know you, Lady Rose. I think you are a much better woman than I have ever been or could ever hope to be." The words made Rose color.

"Oh, no, I'm not good at all. Truly. I have a bad temper and I'm impatient and judgmental and sometimes regardless of my mother's instruction I make very unkind comments about people. I don't have anything close to the quiet and gentle spirit that the Scriptures commend and is so in vogue and admired in a female. I'm hopeless, quite hopeless, and what makes it worse is that I don't care, don't give a fig, and do not even attempt to improve my character." For the moment, Rose felt all her flaws quite deeply. The Baroness chuckled.

"That is all most certainly true, but I assure you it is what your friends find most attractive about you. I have ordered my own carriage to follow you so you can hurry the children over to me without needing to explain anything to your own coachman. You will not want to be late for your party tonight, and I will take such good care of our charges that you may dance the night away without a care for them."

Later, the children hustled down the back steps and into the Baroness's carriage and with a kiss to two cheeks—not Ernie's, of course, he wouldn't hear of it and recoiled as if Rose threatened him with a hot cinder—Rose went back inside.

"Did I hear activity?" asked Alice. She came to the foot of the stairs as Rose was ascending to the now empty second floor. Rose shook her head

"Just me, cousin. I visited the Baroness, who is leaving soon for Lancashire. I didn't want her to leave without saying goodbye. I like her very much."

"Yes," Alice replied but her tone was tinged with curiosity. "She maintains her air of mystery, though, doesn't she? No one I ask seems to know anything about her or recognize her name or understand how she came to have property in England. Of course, the Malarkeys met her on the continent but it wasn't a relationship of either depth or longevity and they were as surprised as anyone else to see her step into town life with the confidence of someone that belonged here. A lovely person, I agree, but really, it is peculiar in a way, don't you think?"

"Nonsense," said Rose, picking up her skirts and turning back to the stairs. "She is French," the observation enough to answer any question and squelch any speculation.

"Well, yes, perhaps that's all it is," Alice murmured unconvinced, but Rose had already disappeared up the stairs. For her the conversation, annoying at best, was over.

That evening with Rose's toilette complete, Carmine stepped back to clap her hands and say, "Oh, Miss, you are a picture. The image of your mother but with your father's eyes, and I think they'd agree that you've never looked better. Aren't you a beauty?" The rhetorical question brought an unladylike frown to the face of its subject.

"I have never been a beauty and I never will be. Look at these dark brows and this wide mouth. There's nothing rosebud in shape or color about me and that's all the fashion this year." She had the unbidden memory of a voluptuous woman with very fair hair, a perfectly bowed mouth, exotic eyes, and skin like white satin.

"Fashion is fickle," Carmine said with the wisdom of her years, "and changes with the seasons. Real beauty is constant."

"You've become a philosopher, Carmine, and I appreciate the sentiment." Rose twirled before the glass so that her skirts swirled out around her. After pleading on Carmine's part, Rose had condescended to wear the cursed bustle and as odd an adornment as she thought it was, it did make her look stylish. The aquamarines set in blush gold lay against her skin and picked up its rosy glow. "I think I will do, after all," she said finally, adjusted the plume that was thrust carefully into her soft hair, and picked up the shawl from the chair. "Thank you, Carmine, and don't wait up."

"No, Miss." But, of course, she would wait up, had done so for years, worried when her young lady was out too far into the morning hours, thrilled to hear all the details of every elegant evening—not enough elegant evenings of late but perhaps that was about to change—and always had her lady's nightdress all laid out, ready to scoot her to bed when she finally did get in. When a husband eventually took his place in the picture, Carmine supposed the routine would change but young or old, married or not, Rose would always be her lady and she would always wait up.

Chloe Fitzhugh greeted Rose and Alice at the door almost as if she had been waiting for them. She knew Alice through their husbands' political relationship but not terribly well and she had never met Lady Rose Carlisle. Chloe came forward, however, with the welcome of a long-time friend, smiling and exuding good humor with her frank, friendly smile.

"I've heard so much about you, Lady Rose," Chloe said to Rose after greeting Alice, "and all of it complimentary. I didn't know you were so beautiful, though. What a lovely gown!" Chloe Fitzhugh had a way about her of making a person feel at home, Rose thought, a gift, really, and despite her recent aversion for blonde curls, which Chloe possessed in abundance, Rose liked her right off.

There was a splendid orchestra with people on the dance floor and already a little queue of potential partners lining up to fill in Rose's card. She supposed that should have been enough to presume an entertaining and enjoyable evening, but she found herself looking around the room, a little unsettled and somewhat disappointed although none of the emotions showed on her face. A woman of inherent honesty, she knew exactly for whom she searched and it was not Oswald Sweete-Cotton. Unfortunately, the man appeared before her like a figure from a recurring bad dream.

"I say, Lady Rose, you look especially well tonight. Is it too much to hope that you would honor me with a dance?" He put out his arm for her to take and stood poised, waiting for her acquiescence.

Next to Rose, John Merton said with casual and insincere regret, "Rough luck, Sweete-Cotton, that you should ask for what is already promised," and to Rose added with nothing casual, insincere, or regretful in his tone, "or am I mistaken, Lady Rose? I feel certain that I requested and you kindly agreed to the first waltz of the evening."

That," said Rose, "is exactly the way I recall it, your grace." She took his arm, feeling suddenly light-hearted, the unsettling, niggling anxiety she had experienced since her arrival at the Fitzhughs' completely vanished.

Walking away, John whispered so only she could hear, “Goose,” causing Rose to catch her breath on a giggle and discreetly turn it into a cough.

“I’ll give you the benefit of the doubt and assume you are not referring to me,” she said.

“Never. That would be ungallant and inexact, as well. You don’t look at all goosish this evening.”

“Opposed to other evenings when I do?” Her tone was teasing with just the slightest edge that she regretted as soon as the words were out of her mouth.

John went on as if she had not spoken, “You look like your namesake on a summer day, all blush and blue.” He made the compliment without discomfort and Rose received it with equal grace, but inside both experienced feelings that were neither comfortable nor graceful, a kind of exhilaration and a rough happiness that did not show on his face at all and crept only a little into the glow on her cheeks. They had been years on the social scene and learned public composure at their fathers’ knees.

For John, the compliment was not nearly as fulsome as he would have wished. Rose truly was beautiful to him. It was not just the blue of the gown, a shade deeper than her eyes and very becoming, or the way her hair was swept up onto her head, soft, richly brown, and complemented by a plume that curved just so under her ear and against her cheek, or the sparkle at her throat that drew attention to her aristocratic neck and smooth, white shoulders. It was more than that—the clear and forthright gaze under those elegantly arched dark brows, her ready, generous smile, the way she held herself tall and proud without seeming in the least arrogant or supercilious, the mischief that always bubbled just below the surface, her ready sense of the ridiculous, her wonderful ability to laugh even at herself without fear of social censure. Holding Rose during the dance, John was so wrapped up in his thoughts of her that he missed much of her initial conversation and was only brought to attention by the words *Rat Catcher.*

“I beg your pardon.”

“That’s his name. Rat Catcher.”

“Whose name?”

"Oh, dear, I fear I've lost my ability to converse intelligibly since it's apparent you haven't heard a word I said." But she spoke with a smile and began the story of the previous evening's confrontation in the hallway again. This time John paid strict attention, his frown deepening with the telling.

"Carmine was the only one to show any sense at all," he told Rose finally, managing to dance with his usual competence while he scolded. "You should have contacted the authorities immediately and worried about explaining the children later. The idea of you coming face to face with such a man chills my blood. I know men like that, know them better than I wish, and you were and are foolish to take him and his threats lightly." Rose, recognizing the sincere concern in his voice, did not take offense at a tone she would ordinarily have tolerated from only her father or brothers.

Instead, she cocked her head to look up at him and ask thoughtfully, "How could you possibly know men like that, your grace? I can't imagine you move in the same circles."

Without thinking he responded, "I spend part of my week in Bluegate Fields, Lady Rose, and have seen the violent results of men exactly like the one you describe."

"You inhabit the East End? Whatever for?" Rose thought she knew why, recalled her cousin mentioning something about the doctor's charity but she wanted to hear it from his own lips. For a reason she could not explain, it was important that she see his face as he answered her seemingly innocent query.

A slight flush of embarrassment crept onto John's cheekbones, and he clearly wished he had never mentioned his forays into the East End. Rose could tell he was searching for a way to explain his activity that did not sound pretentious or self-righteous and saw from his expression how very reluctant he was to speak of his work with the poor at all. Not from a sense of shame, Rose deduced, but from modesty. It said something about the man that he would rather hide his light under a bushel than be credited for good works about which lesser men might boast.

As John searched for the right tone and words to share his passion for the less fortunate, Rose realized with the bright clarity of a summer day that she loved the man. She supposed she may have done so from the very beginning, from the moment she heard his voice disperse the crowd or saw him gently examine Piper with his strong, long-fingered hands as tender as a mother's touch, but it was now, at this very moment, that she knew there would never be another man for her in all her life, knew she would take him on any terms even if his heart was set on another. If she couldn't have his grace, Dr. John Merton, fifth Duke of Quill, Rose knew she would have no one at all. She thought it likely however, from one or two expressions she had caught on his face recently that she would have him and sooner rather than later, once she got him past the regrettable grief that lingered from his mother's abandonment and the more improbable heartbreak he had felt years ago when his Penelope, so inaccurately named from the classics, had faithlessly preferred another. All this introspection passed quickly through her mind as she waited to hear John's response.

"I do a little work there now and then when time allows," he said finally.

"Medical work?"

"Yes. I have the time so why not?" It was all John would say for he quickly changed the subject and the dance ended at the same time. Rose was forced to thank him and allow herself to be propelled back to a chair on the side of the room where an admiring young man waited for her begging the next dance. When she turned to speak to him, John murmured something she did not catch and melted away into the crowd.

Rose watched John carefully all evening without giving the slightest indication that she was doing so, saw that he danced only with his cousin Chloe and her cousin Alice before he drifted back to her side. It pleased her that despite the obvious interruptions by any number of unmarried young women angling for his attention, he did not seem a bit interested in any of them. Rose had spent the past minutes measuring what it would take to overcome John's reluctance to become attached to a woman again and trying to gauge how tender his heart really was. What had been a severe wound and what only hurt pride? She would eventually come to a decision and based on her conclusion would put a plan in place. Rose had a plan for everything, after all, and this, her future happiness—*their* future happiness—necessitated her most well thought out and properly implemented strategy. There was a lifetime at stake.

By the end of the evening, Rose had shared with John the children's move to the home of the Baroness and their departure within the month to Lancashire.

"I rather hate to see it all end," she concluded wistfully. "It made the stay in London bearable and now what will I do with the next month until my parents return and we go home to Cornwall?"

Her rhetorical question brought John up short. He had known in an entirely superficial and intellectual way that Rose was in town only for a visit and not a very long visit at that, but to hear her talk about returning to Cornwall within a month—Cornwall, practically the other end of the world—startled him. He supposed she would have to go, it was her home, and he would go back to his life the way it had been before her—his consuming work, evenings before the fire with Rathbone for company, holidays with Chloe and her family, everything exactly the way it had been before he had spied a chestnut-haired young woman kneeling in the street with blood staining her pretty jacket and her hat knocked askew. The idea of Rose in Cornwall and he in London for the rest of their lives caused a disconcertingly sharp pang of unhappiness and without thinking he frowned down at her as he had done more than once before. By now accustomed to her partner's suddenly stern face, Rose ignored his expression.

"I expect time will pass quickly enough," she continued, "and I do love Cornwall. My brother Robbie says it suits my undisciplined and ill-mannered nature, and I daresay he's right, but my sister loves Cornwall, too, and she is the sweetest tempered, most forgiving person in the world. Goodness knows she had enough virtuous practice growing up with me." The music stopped. "The evening is over, I think. Thank you, your grace, for both the first and the last dance." And all the dances in between, she thought, and the conversation and the lemonade and the laughter and everything about you that is so endearing, even the frowns, but she said none of that and all that was on her face was a polite smile.

He met her smile and lost the unconscious glower that had settled on his brow as he contemplated Rose's departure.

"It was my pleasure, Lady Rose, and now here are your cousin and my cousin to shoo us out the door." There was polite talk a while longer and then good-byes. Rose threw a shawl of dark blue over her shoulders and followed after Alice but turned at the last moment to smile at both John and Chloe, who stood watching her departure.

"Lady Rose is utterly charming, John," said Chloe with the familiarity and affection of many years. "I had heard she was something of a rebel and strong-minded besides, but she's lovely and I would guess very kind. I saw her talking to old Mrs. Fortinbras with unrelenting patience and apparent great interest, although you and I both know how Mrs. Fortinbras tells the same stories over and over, each time as if she is telling them for the first time. Lady Rose never blinked an eye through it all." She caught herself from saying *your* Lady Rose only at the last minute.

Chloe Fitzhugh, one year her cousin's junior and certainly not a renowned doctor, was much more savvy about the human heart than he. She had heard vague rumors about John and Lady Rose Carlisle and invited them both this evening to see the state of his interest for herself. She was satisfied. Not that there had been the slightest misstep by either of them, both pleasant but not in each other's pockets, enjoying each other's company but not exclusively or at the expense of propriety, everything very correct and polite. Chloe still knew she was not mistaken. A love match in the making, she thought, if only her cousin, who had once saved her life and whom she dearly loved, could get past the inconstancy of that dreadful Penelope. What a relief it had been to all of the family—except John, of course—when she had thrown him over for Fountain! An answer to prayer, really, although in the incomprehensible way even highly intelligent men sometimes acted John had not been able to see his good fortune and had withdrawn into a semi-isolated and dull life. Such a waste when he was so fine a man, patient and good-humored and perfectly suited to be a wonderful husband and father. Chloe's husband came up behind her and caught the tail end of her comments to John.

Taking his wife's hand in his with proprietary affection he asked, "Lady Rose Carlisle is related to Abby and William somehow, isn't she?"

"William is her mother's brother," John answered absently, still watching the doorway as if he hoped Rose would suddenly reappear.

"I thought there was a connection, but she doesn't favor William that I can see."

"Not physically, perhaps, but she has his sense of adventure," was John's response. Then he kissed his cousin on the cheek and made his farewell to her and her husband.

Despite instructions, Carmine was waiting up for her mistress when Rose stepped into her room, dropped her shawl into a chair, and said, "You didn't need to wait up, but oh, Carmine, since you did, please, please, please help me out of this corset. One more minute and I will die, and I do not exaggerate. The things we women do for vanity's sake." Rose slipped out of her dress, inhaling deeply and exhaling into a sigh, then thrust her head into the nightgown Carmine held for her.

"So, Miss, was it very lovely and did you have the opportunity to dance? Who was there? Anyone I know? Did that Mrs. Fitzhugh play the harp? I hear she's like an angel with it." Carmine, hanging the blue gown, did not see the expression on Rose's face.

"Yes. Yes. Many people. Several people. No. And yes, she looks and acts like an angel even without a harp." Rose's tone was distracted enough to draw Carmine's attention, who surprised a pensive, serious expression on Rose's face.

"Is everything all right, Miss?"

Rose gave a distracted smile, stuck her feet under the covers, stretched out comfortably with both hands under her head, and stared at the ceiling, thinking.

"Oh yes," she answered finally. "Right as rain."

Carmine, by now used to the vagaries of her young lady, came over to blow out the lamp.

"Well, that's good and I'm glad you had a good time. I can't imagine there was a young man there who didn't fall in love with you on the spot, you looked so pretty."

"That," said Rose meditatively from the darkness, "remains to be seen."

Chapter 8

When Rose awoke the next morning, she by habit started down the hallway to see how Piper and Evie—and perhaps Ernie; his overnight stays were infrequent—had slept. She caught herself as she reached for her own door handle, stopped, and gave a literal shake of her head. Safe and sound, she thought to herself, and why she trusted the Baroness to keep her word she couldn't have explained, only knew that she was a woman who would do as she promised whatever happened.

Over a late breakfast Alice said, "Wasn't it a lovely evening? If ever there was a perfect couple, it's Charles and Chloe Fitzhugh, both so lively and intelligent and doting on each other it's clear to see. Did you enjoy yourself, dear?"

Rose, with an appetite only for strong coffee, answered, "Yes, I did. I didn't know what to expect, but Chloe Fitzhugh reminded me of both Mother and Aunt Abby in her ability to put people at ease. The music was wonderful and except for the bother of that nincompoop Oswald Sweete-Cotton it was a perfect evening." Rose looked over at her cousin with a not entirely attractive guilty look. "I suppose Mother would scold if she heard me talk like that."

"You must never have heard your mother discourse on the subject of her distant cousin Walter. I imagine she would have some sympathy for you regarding Mr. Sweete-Cotton, but regardless of provocation your mother was always correct in her public behavior."

"I am, too," protested Rose and at a silent look from Alice added, "most of the time." She paused. "Except when I'm not." Both women laughed out loud.

"The great difference is that your mother had responsibility forced on her at an early age, Rose, but you have gone looking for it always with an eye out for someone to rescue. I wonder where that fervor comes from. There aren't any Methodists in the family that I know of." Alice's comment moved the conversation to religion and then on to politics. "I'll be glad when Mayhew is home again. I heard from him yesterday and he says another fortnight at the longest so I expect him about the same time your parents are back from their trip. Having you here has been such good company, and I will be glad to tell Mayhew you proved him wrong."

Rose raised both brows. "About—?"

"Mayhew said you could not stay in town for six weeks without rescuing and foisting some poor street child on to another unsuspecting family member. He was worried that it was our turn and admonished me quite firmly not to yield to pity or threats. I am relieved it did not come to either confrontation."

"Mayhew has a very suspicious mind."

"I suspect," answered Alice placidly, "it is a natural effect of so many years in the political arena. Mayhew was the most trusting of young men when we were first married, but with the constant exposure to politicians and the government over the years it is no wonder he has become rather wary in his interactions."

Rose, finally hungry enough for toast and reaching for the marmalade, commented, "It's a great pity if that's true, Alice, because there is an enormous opportunity for men in government to improve the lives of needy people. I wonder if we will see women voting and standing for office in our lifetime."

Alice looked shocked. "Oh, surely not. Women haven't the temperament for such serious business, I'm afraid."

"Stuff and nonsense," Rose responded but her mouth was full of toast and the words came out in an unintelligible mumble. "Mark my words, women will vote and sit in Parliament and practice law—"

"And practice medicine, too?" Alice asked with sly intent and was satisfied by the small splash of pink that fell across

Rose's cheeks. Only someone who knew her very well would have noticed it at all.

"Yes, that, too. Why not? Haven't women cared for the sick throughout the centuries?" Rose pushed herself away from the table. "I am off to see the Baroness today, cousin, and then must stop to get new dancing slippers. I live so riotous a life that I have nearly worn a hole in one toe."

"I thought the Baroness was headed out of town and you already made your farewells."

After a quick recovery, Rose said, "She is, of course, but not until the end of the week and I wish to ask her something about France."

"Do you plan a trip to France in the near future?"

"No, not in the *near* future exactly."

"Mayhew and I spent part of our honeymoon trip in Paris," Alice said. "Did you know?"

"I wasn't born at the time, cousin, so no, I did not."

"I recommend France as a delightful honeymoon destination, my dear." Alice enjoyed the continuing color in Rose's cheeks but took pity on her and ended with the prosaic instruction. "You will take Carmine with you today, of course."

Rose gave a grimace but nodded, aware of the proprieties and her responsibilities and not one to avoid either of them purposefully, however much they might chafe.

Alice stared fixedly at the door through which Rose exited, deep in thought. Unless she was mistaken, and she seldom was about this sort of thing, Robert and Claire could very well return from the Paris Exhibition to find a prospective son-in-law waiting in the wings and a duke at that, an upright young man of impeccable breeding, good habits, and from all reports an enormous fortune, besides. He had inherited several estates from his father, including the family seat in County Quill, Kent, and that classic house he kept in town, and an even greater legacy from his grandparents on his mother's side. Wouldn't that be a triumph if the match came to fruition, especially since it had happened on her watch? Alice had always harbored the suspicion that her Uncle Robert thought her a bit of a ninny, and it would be very pleasant to prove him wrong.

While Rose made frequent trips to visit the children at the Baroness's over the next few days, all of them unknown to

Alice, John lay low, unsure of his own feelings and even more unsure of how and whether to act on them. On the one hand, he could not contemplate Rose's departure for Cornwall without a feeling of despair. He found the thought of returning to his solitary life almost unbearable. How had he managed to live without adventure all these years, without social interaction and laughter, without the vision of clear blue eyes and the very faint, tantalizing fragrance of lily of the valley? And yet, and yet~ It would be a very safe life when Rose was gone, no threat of rejection or disappointment or grief, no fear that she would eventually lose interest, no misgivings that perhaps he really was a dull stick in the mud, a man like his father who'd been concerned only with his own dignity and had alienated those closest to him with his self-righteous prosing and fear of ridicule. So while Rose visited the Baroness's stylish home, played with the children, and walked with the still silent Evie to the park to feed the ducks and admire the flowers, John contemplated the future and struggled with the past.

They met unexpectedly at the front door of the Baroness's home, Rose on her way out and John on his way in, both surprised and secretly thrilled to see the other, their mild and pleasant greetings revealing none of the inner delight that threatened to bubble its way into the conversation with every word.

"Hello, your grace. How nice to see you! Are you here for the Baroness? She is not at home, I'm afraid."

Rose wore a silk dress the color of creamy coffee with a softly draping overskirt one shade darker. She had on a little hat, tip-tilted and lavishly trimmed with small cream-colored flowers. John thought she looked enchanting but not knowing how to tell her so without too much admiration creeping into his voice paid no compliment.

"She asked me to stop by and take a final look at the children before they left for the country." John looked down at the little girl holding tightly to Rose's hand. "Hello, Evie. You're looking very pretty today." She was, too, all in soft yellow with a dainty white collar at her throat.

"I told her that, as well. See, Evie, the doctor agrees with me. Yellow is just the color for you. With your green eyes you look exactly like a cheerful daffodil." Evie smiled at the compliment, those green eyes glowing, but said nothing. There was a pause as both adults awaited a response, and when none came Rose added easily, "We were just going for a walk to the park. Won't you join us, your grace?"

He started to beg off when he felt a little hand tug at his sleeve and looked down to find Evie's eyes turned up to him with a clear request despite her silence. Even if he'd really wanted to resist, which he didn't, one look at that little face would have convinced him to change his mind.

"I'd like that very much," he said and turned back down the front steps to follow Rose and Evie. Behind him, Carmine slipped out the front door to join them, her expression one of mute apology. Lady Rose needs a chaperone, her look said, and I don't make the rules, only follow them. John smiled his understanding.

"We have not seen you in several days," Rose commented, using the plural to camouflage the fact that she was the one who had missed seeing him.

"I stay busy," John responded and because he thought the terse statement sounded somewhat churlish added, "I hope you have been spared any more unpleasant hallway confrontations."

"Yes, indeed. We sleep the sleep of the innocent. Besides, Forsythe assures me that everything is double locked and we are as safe as the queen's gems." They walked side-by-side chatting with companionable ease, the late spring sunshine welcome and warming. Evie, caught between them, reached up and grasped a hand of each in hers. It startled, then pleased John, who felt as if he had just been turned into a family without realizing it.

Once at the park, Carmine went off with Evie to visit the ducks on the pond and John and Rose sat on a bench to watch them.

"Will she ever speak, do you think?" Rose asked, watching the happy little girl crouch at the water's edge holding out a hand to one of the ducks.

"Yes, I think so. Something will happen to make her forget the distress that paralyzes her voice and then I believe she will speak."

"Ernie says it was losing their mother that caused the condition. I'm thankful I cannot speak from experience, but I don't doubt that losing one's mother at an early age could deeply distress a child." Rose did not turn to look at him as she spoke but continued to watch Carmine and Evie stroll around the pond.

John turned to give her profile a quick look but saw nothing leading or suspicious there. How could she know, he asked himself with his usual obliviousness to the power and longevity of gossip. Rose would have been a toddler in Cornwall at the time and why would his family's past have come up during this London visit?

"Yes, it can be distressing." She turned to fix a steady gaze on him.

"You sound peculiarly certain. Have I said something inappropriate? I didn't mean to stir up painful memories."

Instead of responding the doctor leaned forward, clasping his hands and resting his elbows on his knees, to stare ahead at nothing in particular. This time it was Rose's turn to examine his profile.

"Apparently, I have over stepped. Please forgive me."

"I lost my mother when I was nine." His bleak tone touched her heart and her reply was quick and sincere.

"I'm so sorry. How horrid that must have been for you!" She knew the story from Alice but asked nevertheless, "Was it a fever? When I was ten I caught something pestilential and very nearly didn't recover myself. Your mother must have been very young. What a terrible grief for you and your father!" He did not speak for a long time, only sat as silent as Evie, staring ahead lost in private thought.

Finally, John said, "My mother ran away and my father divorced her not long afterwards. I'm told it was quite the scandal at the time. I haven't heard or seen from her since, not in twenty years, and I don't know if she is alive or dead to this day. After she left, my father never spoke her name and would not allow me to ask about her."

"I'm sure that was devastating for a little boy. Your father must have loved her very much to carry such a bitter load all those years and to force that load onto your shoulders, as well." John, surprised, turned to look at Rose's sympathetic face.

"Yes, I think he did love her in his way, loved her as much as he was able. Most people didn't understand that and thought it was his pride or his arrogance that caused his unnatural reticence, but I know it was grief. He was not a man easily given to showing or sharing his emotion, but I believe he missed her very much."

"As did you." A statement John did not, could not, refute.

"Yes, as did I."

After a moment Rose asked, "What was she like then, your mother? Do you remember anything about her?"

No one since his cousins' cousin Abby, many years before, had asked him about his mother, not even his closest friends and certainly not Penelope, who was only interested in the past if it had a direct and financial bearing on her future. He was glad of the question, though, and responded almost eagerly.

"She was very young when she wed my father, not even eighteen yet, and I was born before she was twenty. My father removed all the images of her from the house at her abandonment but I can recall her bright smile of mischief. She liked to sing all sorts of songs, too, I remember. Some of them made me laugh."

"Sailors and mermaids," murmured Rose and he gave her a quick, appreciative look.

"Yes, sailors and mermaids. I remember her singing that song to me when I was very little and she would come to tuck me into bed. She was very gay and given to talking in extremes, expressive in all respects and prone to laughter. When I was very little and would skin my knee or be frightened of the dark, she would snatch me up and whisper in my ear, 'Don't cry. It will be all right. Don't cry, John.' She had a voice like music and it always comforted. I thought her the best and most beautiful mother in the world." He felt suddenly embarrassed that he had said so much and stood. "Here comes your little charge looking wet around the edges." It was true. The hem of Evie's skirt looked much the worse for wear.

"She was determined to follow the little fuzzy duckling into the water," Carmine explained with a complacent smile. Rose stood, too.

"And did you catch it, Evie?" The child, afraid of a scolding, shook her head, the apprehensive look on her face affecting Rose so deeply that she leaned to give the little girl a kiss on the forehead. "Well, too bad for you but fortunate for the little duck. No doubt it is back with its mother by now. Don't worry about your skirts. They will dry. It's only water."

"I must get back." John was still somewhat embarrassed by his surfeit of confidences. What had come over him to reminisce with that degree of feeling?

"May we walk with you? We won't stay any longer, either. Evie should get home and put on dry clothes."

Rose, very aware of the doctor's discomfort, took a light tone and asked John if he had a refuge in the country to which he retired during the peak London heat. He began to speak about his country home in Kent and after a short while was himself again. Later he would remember with appreciative admiration the kind ease with which Rose had distracted him and think that her genuine kindness was one of her most attractive features. One among so many, of course. Chestnut hair that showed gold in the sun and those wonderful eyes were not far behind on the list.

Rose was so preoccupied at supper that evening that Alice had to ask her the same question more than once. The brief conversation in the park had told Rose more than John could possibly have guessed, had touched her heart in a curiously tender way and it had been all she could do to keep from putting her arms around him and drawing his head down to her shoulder. The thought of his expression had she done so would almost have been worth it, Rose thought, smiling to herself. Alice noticed the smile and guessed at a reason. Had she known it, she was not far off the mark.

Two days later Rose was back at the Baroness's and this time the older woman was at home. Rose descended from her carriage, waved Peek away, and met the Baroness at the front door.

"We should take advantage of the good weather, Baroness. It is so perfect that I thought I might borrow Piper and Evie for a walk." If Rose had told the truth, she would have admitted that she was restless and strangely unhappy, impatient, unable to stay focused, given to pacing, and desirous of something unformed and as yet unnamed. She confessed to nothing of the sort, however, but for Rose to appear at the Baroness's doorstep without Carmine doing chaperone duty was rare and unwise. The Baroness recognized it as such.

"But, Lady Rose, I cannot accompany you and I have sent Giselle on an errand."

"It's only to the park, Baroness, and I will have both the children as company. Surely no one can find fault with that. I will be in full view of the world the whole time and I promise to be gone no longer than an hour. It is much too pretty to stay inside." Rose wore such a humble and importunate expression that the Baroness, against her better judgment, agreed.

"But no longer than one hour or I shall worry."

"The park is inhabited by the most benign ducks and pigeons. In your lovely neighborhood I am convinced we shall be quite safe." But this was one of those rare occasions when Rose was profoundly mistaken.

With Ernie out and about on his own adventure—even the Baroness's good intentions could not restrain Ernie when he chose to ramble—Rose promised Piper and Evie a walk through the park clear to the other side where a seller of hokey-pokey was situated against the curb. Hokey-pokey, a cold, sweet, creamy confection, was all the rage in town and Rose carried a little purse with her that jangled with coins for the express purpose of partaking of the popular ambrosia. Both children were excited. Evie, dressed again in her favorite yellow, held tightly to Rose's hand and Piper skipped up ahead. All three companions enjoyed the greening park and abundant flowers and all three, even Rose with a latent sweet tooth, anticipated the smooth, cool treat on their tongues. They found the hokey-pokey man right away and waited in the short line for their treats.

As Rose turned toward the man to open her purse and rummage around for the proper coins, the children intent on their icy delicacies wandered a short distance up the curb and along the street. Because it was later in the afternoon, there was not much of a crowd and Rose leisurely counted the amount due into the man's hand when she heard a cry, heard its beginning and its sudden interruption, exactly the way a cry would sound if someone clapped a hand over the crier's mouth. Her own hand trembled as the sound registered and she whirled around, looking in desperation for the children. With horror and outrage she found them. Little Evie was thrust under the burly arm of the man Rose had met in the hallway several nights before and with his other hand, the Rat Catcher grappled with Piper, who to his credit put up a struggle worthy of someone twice his size.

"You! You there! Release those children at once!" Rose cried and ran toward them. Her sudden call caused the man to lose his grip on Piper, who broke free and turned to give the man a swift, hard kick in the shins. Rose saw the assailant pull back his fist to strike the boy and rushing forward she exclaimed in a loud, stern, and carrying voice, "Don't you dare strike that child! Don't you dare!" Rat Catcher, the blow arrested, hesitated, gave Piper a shove so that the boy fell to his knees, and with a squirming Evie tucked firmly under his arm ran down the walk toward a waiting cab. Rose stopped for only the barest moment by Piper.

"Ernie must know where his lair is," she panted. "Go back immediately to the Baroness and tell her what has happened. Find Ernie and Dr. Merton and tell them, too. I won't lose Evie, I promise." Piper watched Rose's back as she hurried down the street after the kidnapper.

"But Lady Rose—" Piper was afraid for his sister and uncertain what he should do, only aware that there was danger all around.

"Go! Now! Do as I say and hurry, Piper! Everything rests on you. Be sure to tell the doctor."

She shouted that last bit over her shoulder and stopped at a near hansom cab. Piper heard her call up to the yellow-coated driver, "See that cab just pulling away? There's an extra shilling for you if you follow it wherever it goes. I don't care where or what part of the city, just don't lose it. If you do, I will have your hack as forfeiture."

The aristocratic tone of Rose's voice made her serious intention obvious. She climbed in without assistance and the hansom cab pulled away to disappear into the crowd of traffic. Piper hesitated not even a second. Both his ladies were gone and he was determined not to fail them. For all his young years, the boy had the wisdom to realize that Lady Rose was right—everything did indeed rest on him.

Inside the cab, Rose did not give a thought to anything but the shocking incident and the condition of her small, silent charge. How long had the entire kidnapping taken? Five minutes at most? Had any passerby noticed the altercation and if noticed, would anyone care? The streets of London were full of all sorts of wickedness and people had learned to turn a blind eye to most of it.

Rose could not forget Evie in the brawny grip of that monstrous man, her little face pale and frightened, beating against her captor's back with childish fists, blows that must have felt like nothing more than tiny taps to one so powerful. Rose honestly thought she could have killed the man when she saw him draw back his fist, would have done it without a pang if she'd had a weapon at hand. Not that she knew the first thing about firearms—hunting and hounds not being a pastime during her Cornwall childhood—but she was quick and what was there to know, anyway? Aim and pull the trigger and hope for the best.

Now to think of the mute little girl at the mercy of such a villain made her shudder. Rose drew a deep breath, took strength and calm from the knowledge that she was Evie's only hope, and did her best to concoct a plan of sorts. She trusted that her driver kept up because the clip clop of the horse's hooves remained steady, and Rose had no doubt their destination would be a place she was unused to frequenting. It would be wise to ensure that the young woman who climbed out of the cab was not the same young woman who had climbed in. An easy enough transformation if one put one's mind to it.

By the time the cab stopped, the sight of the person that disembarked made the cabbie gape in astonishment. He was certain he'd had a young and presentable lady inside, but who was this woman exiting, hair disheveled and pulled back with a scarf, skirt torn, dirt along her chin, and a shawl tied around her skirt like an apron?

"Here, now," the cabbie said, his eyes narrowed with suspicion, "where's the lady with my fare? She promised me an extra shilling, she did, and I never lost the cab what she told me to follow."

He caught both coins that flew through the air, gave them a quick look, and pocketed them.

"Where'd they go then?" this woman asked, her accent from the East End recognizable and her chin jutting in a look that promised argument if he didn't give an acceptable answer.

"Down that lane," he gestured, still puzzled. They looked to be the same blue eyes he'd seen briefly at the beginning of the ride but he was sure of nothing else. The scruffy woman shot him a scornful look, rubbed her hand against the dirty side of the cab and darkened her cheeks even more from the dirt there, and let her skirts trail in the filthy street as she followed where he pointed. No lady there, he thought, watching her walk flat-footed and ungracefully away from him, but later he found a pretty little capote hat with green silk ribbon ties and a lace fichu, exquisitely made even to his uneducated eyes, on the seat of his cab and wondered if he was mistaken, after all.

Rose had only heard of Bluegate Fields, but she had no doubt that was where she'd been deposited. There could be no other place so vile, its squalor and stench legendary, listless pockets of apathetic people bunched on the corners, everyone and everything dark with dirt and disease and hopelessness. She knew in some practical and functioning part of her mind that she should be frightened, but she was fueled with such outrage and anger that she could not seem to work up any worthwhile fear. Far down the lane she kept track of the Rat Catcher's bobbing head in the fading light and saw him turn abruptly and disappear. For a moment she panicked, picked up her pace and grew careless, running smack into a hefty woman that began to berate Rose's clumsiness in a loud voice.

Rose's hands clenched in fear and frustration on the knot of the shawl tied at her waist and the woman, seeing Rose's fists, stopped in the middle of her tirade to ask roughly, "What's your problem then?"

"He took my girl."

"Who?"

"Don't know. A big man with burly arms snatched her off the street. Took my Evie, he did. I saw him turn in there." The woman looked to where Rose pointed and then back at her.

"Him," the one word ominous." There was silence between them as the big woman examined Rose carefully. "You don't belong here," she stated finally.

"Neither does my Evie." Rose refused to be cowed. The woman's shrewd eyes came to a decision and she gave a nod.

"He got her for the mines up north, no doubt. I heard he was shipping out a load of kiddies to the coal mines tomorrow.

He takes the smallest ones that fit in the spaces where a grown man won't. Mine owners can't get enough of 'em." She spit on the ground. "Them fine lords and ladies like their fires hot and their drawing rooms comfortable and if it's done over the bodies of a few poor kiddies, where's the harm?" She put a not unkind hand to Rose's shoulder and turned her into a side doorway. "You hunker down here. Put your head on your arms like the other poor souls you see. Pretend you're sleeping. Don't draw no attention to yourself. I'll take a look inside. No one gets in Peg's way, not even that'n." She tossed her head in the direction of the tall, narrow, filthy building next to them. "Not even him for all he thinks he rules the place. Just wait."

Rose waited. She had no other choice and knew it. The thought of Evie thrust into a hole in the ground, cut off from the sun that she loved, a bright daffodil lost in darkness, helpless and unable to call out or cry for help caused a shudder throughout Rose's body and a catch in her throat. Tears of frustration and outrage welled up in her eyes and spilled over, streaking her cheeks even more. Weary and as close to despairing as she had ever been, Rose did exactly as Peg directed: sat down in the farthest, darkest corner of the dirty doorway, pulled her knees up to her chest, and rested her forehead against her folded arms. Someone will come, she thought, someone will bring Evie to safety, someone will take us both home. Someone is on his way and someone will come, but what Rose meant was, John is on his way and John will come.

Chapter 9

John *was* on his way but he almost wasn't because he nearly missed the message. Years later the memory of how close, how catastrophically close, he had come to being gone from home when Ernie arrived still had the power to turn his face pale. John was on his way out that late afternoon, had, in fact, closed the carriage door and settled back in the seat for some quiet reflection when he heard a young voice—at first not realizing it was Ernie's—cry, "I need the guv! I need him now!"

There was something so piercing, so desperate in the lad's tone that John stuck his head out to see who it was and immediately called to the driver to stop. He hopped out and looked back toward the house, saw Rathbone in the doorway and the boy, now recognizable as Ernie, on the doorstep. A queer sense of urgency made John pick up speed, something he knew deep down but couldn't have said how or why he knew, only that he was certain Rose needed him. His grace was up the steps and by Ernie's side in a minute, not winded in the least thanks to his boxing training and sprinting exercises. All three stepped inside the front door.

"What?" demanded John abruptly.

In hurried but concise language, Ernie told him the story as he'd heard it from Piper. "I was just in myself and he rushes into the house, right up to the Baroness, grabs her hand, and says to get you. Lady Rose told him real particular. Get Ernie and the doctor, she says. They'll know what to do."

For just a minute John stood there helplessly. Know what to do?! He hadn't a clue what to do and didn't know where to start to look for Rose or the child. He couldn't bear to think about what dangers were befalling them even as he stood there in the hallway discussing the situation. Then his doctor's nerves took over. All his training, professional and athletic, calmed his mind and steadied his heart.

"Ernie, do you have an idea where they might be?"

Ernie nodded. "Rookery Lane. That's where he holes up and that's where he'll stash our ladies." The boy had a quirky dignity about him with his thin, fierce face and the same blazing, dark eyes of his younger brother.

"Rathbone," John went on, "contact the authorities immediately on my behalf. Get Inspector Bertram if you can find him. He knows me and will come immediately. Tell him to get to Rookery Lane in the East End. Bluegate Fields, I think. He'll know where it is. He's been there before. Come along, Ernie, our ladies are waiting for us."

The three men scattered, old Rathbone to get word to the inspector and John and Ernie out the door and down to the waiting carriage. They shared a quiet ride. John, his eyes gray as pewter and his expression cool and still, could let his mind wander only so far. He could not picture his Rose, *his* Rose, in danger or afraid or in any situation that might distress her without feeling as if he'd let his opponent land a full blow to the pit of his stomach. It will be all right, he thought, everything will be all right, safe, sound, right as rain, all right. But what he meant was, Rose will be all right.

****

It seemed hours before Peg returned and while Rose knew that to be an exaggeration, it had grown dark enough around her that in the narrow confines of the lane surrounded by dilapidated buildings that blocked the sun it could indeed have been midnight.

She rose when Peg shook her shoulder and the women stood facing each other as Peg said, "She's in there, second floor, last room on the right, and it's rare he's by himself. Be careful, though. Sounds like he's in a right bad temper. You can make it up the steps easy enough but you best wait until you know he's gone."

"All right. Thank you."

Peg shrugged. "I lost a girl once. A boy, too. Hard to get past that."

When the woman walked away, Rose allowed herself a moment to feel bereft and fearful before she turned her attention to the house. She would watch the door all night if she must and would not be deterred, but she hoped it would not really take all night. Even she would be hard pressed to invent an excuse that would explain her being out all night and Alice would be worried sick in the meantime.

Rose was well aware that her reputation would be in shreds if any word of this fantastic and highly questionable escapade leaked out. She contemplated being banished to a quiet future in Cornwall, eccentric sister and spinster aunt, the family oddity. Where once she had viewed such a fate with good-natured stoicism, even a certain proud rebellion, she found she could no longer do so. Something had changed; other hopes and dreams had intervened. But she would not, could not, think of those things now. Instead, she settled back into the dark corner of a dark doorway on a dark street, the daughter of a Marquis and the granddaughter of an Earl huddled with a scarf wrapped tightly around her head and her cheek pressed against her folded arms. Rose made herself as small and still as she could and no one passing gave the shadowed overhang where she waited a second look. Her head was turned so that she had a clear view under the dim, almost macabre lamplight that illumined the doorway of the house next door.

In a surprisingly, pleasingly, short time, Rose saw the ominous silhouette of Rat Catcher step outside into the alley. There was no mistaking that vermin-like head and his forward thrusting gait. He stopped just outside the door, raised his head and sniffed the air like a wild creature. Then hunching his head into his shoulders, he slid into the shadows and disappeared. Rose counted to twenty and crouching in the shadows herself, crept closer, pushed open the door that hung sideways, and stepped inside the decrepit building. It smelled of all sorts of unpleasant things but she did not give that a thought. There were the steps and the prize waited just above her.

The unilluminated interior of the place was black as a moonless night but eventually her eyes adjusted enough to allow her to place one careful foot on each step. She took the stairs as a baby learning its first ascent: one foot up and the other foot to join it, pause, listen, then a foot to the next step and the other up with it again. It was cautious and tedious progress. The last door on the right was closed tightly but a key stuck out of the keyhole. Rose never hesitated but turned the key carefully. It was a well-oiled lock with no forthcoming scrape or squeak. The smooth, silent opening of the door rekindled her outrage, which had been woefully dimmed by the time she'd spent waiting and the little licks of fear she had now and again experienced.

But now—! How many children had that monster locked into this room? How often did he use it that the lock and the hinges were so primed and quiet? How much traffic in helpless human beings went on in this horrible place?

When Rose pushed open the door into the dark room a sound greeted her, a little voice clear and pure, singing a tune teasingly familiar to Rose although she could not at the moment place it.

"Evie? Is that you? It's Lady Rose. Evie?"

At Rose's whisper, the singing stopped abruptly and Rose, barely able to see in the very dim interior, made out the little girl seated on a rickety cot in the corner of the otherwise empty room. Evie sat cross-legged with her pretty daffodil skirts bunched all around her. The child gave a little squeak and was off the bed in a second, her arms outstretched and then wrapped around Rose's knees with the grip of a wrestler. Rose scooped her up and Evie transferred her grasp to Rose's neck, burying her little face into Rose's shoulder and saying her name *Lady Rose Lady Rose Lady Rose* over and over.

The desperate delight of the little girl's murmured welcome made everything Rose had experienced the past hours fade away and at first she hugged her back, saying, "It will be all right now. I'm here." After a moment, however, Rose grew quite still and found her voice to say, "Evie, I heard you. You're talking."

The child nodded. "Yes," Evie said, "I am."

Rose wanted to find out more, why and when and what and how, but she knew her one priority just then was to get out of this nasty house and this nasty place, to get Evie home safe and sound. They could talk, really and truly talk, about the miracle later. Unfortunately, Rose's original plan of action stopped at finding Evie. A secondary plan to get the child out of the East End and back to the Baroness remained not just nebulous but totally non-existent. Still holding the girl—or perhaps, the other way around—Rose waited, figuratively speaking, for inspiration even as she slid back out into the black hallway and crept inch by inch with her back against the damp wall toward where she remembered the rickety steps were. She was conscious of Evie's light breathing against her cheek and for a moment became more focused on comforting the child than on her surroundings and so was completely taken aback, shocked to the point of a little scream, when she ran straight into a figure standing in front of her.

Immediately Rose backed up, turned Evie away from the man—she knew from impact that it was a large, solid man—and said in a voice that possessed only a slight quaver, "Back away, sir. I hold a weapon and have no doubt I will use it if needs be." Rose forgot her East End accent and spoke the words in a cool, aristocratic, and arrogant tone. I am out for a stroll, her tone said, and will not tolerate being inconvenienced.

In response, conscious of a heady relief and something stronger that warred with expediency John said, "Believe me when I say I have no doubt of that, Lady Rose, and if you really do have a weapon, I beg you point it anywhere but straight ahead. Ernie and I would be at risk." Rose gave a great gasp somewhere between a sob and a laugh.

"John," was all she said and found herself, Evie and all, enveloped in his arms, held tightly against him so that she could smell his crisp scent. She thought that in all her life, past or future, she had never before and would never again welcome anything so much as she did the sound of his voice and the warmth of his embrace.

"What an idiot you are!" he said over her ear but the tenderness in his tone contradicted the scolding words.

"Yes, I can't argue with that but listen, John," she had slipped easily into his first name without realizing it, a familiarity he noted and approved, "Evie's speaking. I heard her singing and she said my name."

John was suddenly conscious that he crushed the little girl between them and loosened his hold as Ernie began pulling at his coattail in earnest.

"C'mon, guv. We don't want that one to come back and find us here. It won't matter to him if you're a duke and a lady. He's no one you want to cross."

John reached for Evie, transferred her from Rose's hold to his own, took Rose's hand in his free hand, and started carefully down the steps. Ernie's words brought them suddenly back to the present situation and the two adults became very quiet. Rose, not a woman easily led, was quite content to follow John's lead step by step down the old stairs, each creak a step closer to freedom and home. They reached the bottom of the stairs and made the sharp turn to the broken front door. Ernie pushed open the door and darted out, followed more slowly by John with Evie holding on to his neck with her little arms. Amazingly, he could hear the child humming to herself under her breath although he could not make out the tune. He was also conscious of Rose's hand in his, warm and steady and not a tremble to indicate she was in the middle of the East End surrounded by the threat of its infamous gangs of vice-laden ruffians, hooligans, thieves, pickpockets, and much, much worse. It seemed to be night when they stepped outside with only the queer, flickering gas streetlamp for illumination. John turned to Rose.

"Watch your step. We'll be out of here soon. Are you all right?"

She was conscious of her smudged face, disheveled hair poking all which ways out of her scarf, her tattered and stained skirts, her filthy hands, and felt almost shy with him.

"Yes, I'm fine, just a little tired and now anxious that I've caused Alice to worry."

"Alice," he said not quite under his breath, "was not the only one worrying," and would have said more when out of the dark shadow of the alley in front of them came a voice.

"Where you going with my property?" it said.

John and Rose froze simultaneously and Evie's clutch on John's neck so intensified that he had to reach up and gently loosen her arms so he could swallow.

John pushed Rose behind him as he answered easily, "No property of yours here," and waited, trying to locate the source of the voice in the darkness.

"I bought and paid for that brat you got there and she's mine. You leave her down and you and that other one can go, but you ain't taking my property. No one takes what's rightfully mine." With those words he stepped out of the shadows, a large man with a bristled, rodent-like head and arms that seemed too big for his body. To Rose he seemed perverted and twisted, more like an animal and not human at all.

Without a word and without taking his gaze from the man, John slid Evie back into Rose's arms.

Then he drawled in a cool and scornful voice, "You forget to whom you're speaking, sir. There is nothing here that's rightfully yours and you would be wise to let us pass."

Rose saw something gleam in the pale light. "John, beware! He has a knife," her voice an urgent whisper. "Don't let him get close to you."

The man brandished a long, narrow, two-edged blade that looked dangerous even from a distance, but John did not retreat as Rat Catcher approached. Instead, he placed himself squarely between the advancing man and Rose where she stood holding Evie. The duke faced Rat Catcher with his legs slightly apart, his expression indifferent, his posture casual, and with only a small smile displayed at the approaching menace. Rat Catcher came closer still, walking with that curious posture that seemed so fearful and threatening, something furtive and evil about everything he did. He was close enough for Rose to see the whiskers spraying out from his cheeks when without warning there was a loud, sodden thud and the man fell forward, first onto his knees with the knife flying out of his hands and then flat onto his stomach. His head thudded against the packed ground. Behind him stood Ernie holding a large, flat board in both hands poised to hit the terrible man yet again. He had come up from the rear and landed a blow across the back of Rat Catcher's knees to topple the rat forward.

"Good job, Ernie!" John called and leaped forward to kick the knife well into the dark side alley before he reached for Rose's free hand. "Let's go!"

They all ran then, Ernie tossing the board to the side and leading the way out of the alley and down the black, grimy streets. Coming directly at them was a group of men as purposeful in arriving as John and Rose were in departing.

Rose's first thought was a gang of some sort, who would be as intent on harming them as Rat Catcher had been, but when she looked more closely she breathed a sigh of relief. A gang, perhaps, but a welcome one, three London bobbies led by a man in a tweed coat and derby hat.

"Your grace," the man in the coat panted, "are you all right? I was out and didn't get the message right away." John waved a hand behind him.

"I'm fine, Inspector. There's a man back there who's a bad one, though, someone you've been seeking for a while, I'd wager, the cur that's trafficked in children for years."

"Rat Catcher." Bertram said the name with satisfaction and ordered the other men into the alley to find and hold the criminal in custody. After the bobbies left, he glanced at Rose holding Evie. "Would this be one of his victims, then, sir?"

"Yes, this is Mrs. Greatheart and her girl, Evie. She came to me for help retrieving her daughter."

Rose said in broad cockney, ""e took me Evie, 'e did. I weren't losing 'er to the likes o' 'im." She trailed along behind the two men as they headed out of Bluegate down the filthy streets, past doorways that had quickly emptied with the sudden appearance of the police, and out finally into the light.

Rose was amazed that it was not night, after all. There remained a touch of daylight in the sky; the streets were filled with people out and about; normal life continued. How terrible that people must live in that foul darkness, she thought. Was it any wonder they were dehumanized and brutal surrounded as they were by dirt and stench and constant darkness? She hugged Evie even closer. Not this little one, at least, Rose thought, and gave a little prayer of thanks that they were all—she looked at John's broad back and was conscious of an emotion so intense, so deeply heartfelt that for a moment she feared she would weep—*all* safe and sound and free from that terrible place.

John helped Rose into the carriage, saying to his driver without noticeable emotion and with barely a glance at Rose, "Take Mrs. Greatheart and Evie to the Baroness de Anselme's. I have business with the inspector." The two men walked away, heads bent in discussion with Ernie between them listening to the conversation and nodding as intently as a grown man. No surprise there, for a grown man's heart beat in that wiry little body despite its youth.

After Rose lifted Evie more comfortably into her lap, she lay her head back against the cushion, enjoying the smooth ride of the duke's carriage, and evaluated her life with serious introspection. What she had just been through had certainly been an adventure and it was true that she was used to adventures, liked them and had on occasion even sought them out, but Rose decided it might be wise to take a break from them for a while. She had other plans. At that moment she was certain the only adventure in which she was interested—for the near future and very possibly into the far, far distant future—had to do with the man she loved and who, she now believed, loved her just as dearly.

Contentedly curled in Rose's lap, Evie sang under her breath, "I'm a sailor man and I've sailed the world; / I've floated every ocean with my flag unfurled."

Rose was suddenly intent on the little girl's verses. Something about the song stirred memory and stirred something even more profound: a thought so extraordinary that at first she could not credit it.

"But the sight that set my heart to fail," Evie sang on softly to herself against Rose's chest, "was the vision of a woman with a long, green tail."

"What a funny song! Where did you learn all those words?" Rose asked the child and waited, but she thought she already knew what Evie's answer would be.

"The Baroness taught me," Evie said, so easy with speaking one would never imagine she had been mute for months. "She comes in every night after my bath and sings it to me. Then she says, 'Good night, *mon cherie*.'" Evie spoke the last words just right, mimicking the Baroness's French lilt and giving the words a music all their own.

Oh, my, thought Rose and for the second time that night quick, unbidden tears sprang to her eyes. Oh, my.

Evie finished the verse with a rousing refrain. "O, fish and fin and gill and scale / 'Twas the vision of a woman with a long, green tail." Hearing it, Rose did not know whether to laugh or to cry.

Carmine waited anxiously with the Baroness in the French woman's front parlor, with Piper there, too, all three pale-faced and worried. When Rose with Evie stepped inside the Baroness's front door, the trio swooped around them.

"Oh, Miss," breathed Carmine. Her tone was almost admiring. "If I didn't know it was you, I'd never have known it was you." Strangely enough, Rose understood exactly what Carmine meant by that disjointed sentence and felt a flicker of gratification.

"Yes, I think I rather outdid myself this time, but I will miss that little hat I had to leave in the cab."

The Baroness, more practical, said, "Giselle, take Evie upstairs and give her a good wash and all the cherry cookies she wants for supper. Piper, you go along with your sister while I talk to Lady Rose." Evie planted one more kiss on Rose's cheek before she disengaged her arms from around her rescuer's neck and allowed herself to be led upstairs, the idea of endless cherry cookies already mesmerizing her.

"Are you both all right?" the Baroness asked and at Rose's assurance added, "You were very, very foolish, Lady Rose. What could have happened to you I dare not think." Rose smiled at her.

"I was very, very foolish, I agree, but I could not think of any other way to keep our Evie safe. I realize quite dreadful things could have happened to both Evie and me, but none did and while I am a terrible mess, I am otherwise none the worse for wear. It was all worth it, besides, because the authorities apprehended that monster of a man the children called Rat Catcher."

"I would like to hear more and I am sure I will, but Carmine and I have just barely assuaged your cousin's concerns and you need to get home—*not* looking like that, of course. *Mon Dieu*, your cousin would collapse from palpitations! As soon as I realized you might be gone a while, I sent for Carmine in confidence and followed that by sending a note to your cousin telling her your homecoming might be somewhat delayed because we were engaged in sewing goods for the poor."

"And she believed it?" asked Rose, awe struck. "For anyone who knows my lamentable skill with a needle that news would really stretch the boundaries of credibility."

"Forgive me for not being as quick-witted as you when creating plausible fictions," the Baroness retorted, a tart tone creeping into her voice. "I have not had your experience." Softening, she added, "I do not know if she believed it, but I am sure when you go back to Pembroke Court this evening, you will speak very persuasively about the satisfaction of hours spent sewing for those less fortunate. Now, Carmine, take Lady Rose upstairs to my room where I have laid out a gown that might just do. Work your magic and make her presentable so she will cause no consternation upon her return home, and do it quickly because you were both expected there over an hour ago." As Rose and Carmine started for the stairs, the Baroness asked casually, "Did his grace, Dr. Merton, find you?"

"Yes, he and Ernie arrived just at the right time. Evie and I were never so glad to see anyone in our lives."

"And his grace is safe and well, I hope."

"Yes," answered Rose gently, "very safe and very well."

Carmine tugged Mrs. Greatheart up the stairs to be reworked into Lady Rose Carlisle, daughter of a Marquis and granddaughter, on her mother's side, of an Earl. The transformation was not that difficult for a woman of Carmine's experience and expertise and within a short time Rose said her goodbyes to her hostess and the children and disembarked the Baroness's carriage at her own front door. Forsythe, waiting for her and, Rose was sure, anticipating scandal, opened the door before Rose could reach the handle.

"Lady Rose, you have been gone some time." He eyed her clothes carefully and frowned.

"Yes," she answered with airy disregard, stretching out her arms before her and turning her palms up as if she waited for him to hand her a package. "I have been sewing for the indigent."

"Sewing?" Forsythe repeated, certain he must have misheard. "Sewing what?" Because the incredulity in his tone was palpable and could be considered impertinent, the butler forced himself to conclude with "your ladyship," hoping that adding the title would cover the skeptical disbelief in his voice.

Rose dropped her (borrowed) cape into his hands, perfectly content that he should see it and not recognize it as hers. It would bother him for days. He was an insufferable snob and she refused to allow him to intimidate her.

"Oh, things, you know, scarves and aprons and skirts and under drawers."

She chose her garments with purpose, knowing full well that the idea of her sewing under drawers would be enough to bring on an attack of apoplexy in the butler. In the hall lamp light he did appear to turn a little green around the gills.

Gills. The word turned Rose's attention inward to that silly little ditty of Evie's—O, fish and fin and gill and scale / 'Twas the vision of a woman with a long, green tail. Teasing Forsythe suddenly lost its appeal.

"Where is my cousin, Forsythe?"

"I'm here, Rose." Alice hurried down the hallway from the library. "Goodness, you've been gone a long time! If you hadn't had Carmine with you, I would have been sick with apprehension, though I could have sworn I saw Carmine downstairs after you had already left. Well, I admit time got away from me today and I must be mistaken. I don't mean to be offensive, my dear, but you hate to sew. How did the Baroness ever convince you to do a task you have considered tedious and disagreeable since childhood?"

"She spoke to my conscience," Rose replied, taking care to speak as much of the truth as circumstances allowed. She leaned forward to kiss her cousin on the cheek. "Now let me go upstairs and refresh. Am I too late for supper?"

"It's just being set." Alice paused. "Is that a new gown, Rose? I don't recall seeing it."

"New to you, perhaps, but it's been worn before. I'll be back down to join you in a quarter hour and you can give me the latest news of Mayhew." Alice was happily diverted.

"Oh, it is the best news ever, Rose! I've had a letter and he will be home in a mere week. There's a letter from your parents, as well, who will be back in London about the same time. Won't it be wonderful to have the family all together again? It is just not the same when the people one cares for are distant."

Rose, not thinking of her parents or Mayhew at all, still agreed wholeheartedly with the sentiment.

Chapter 10

Rose slept soundly that night despite the speculative thoughts that raced through her mind and awoke the next morning refreshed and curiously, light-heartedly happy. She had the vague anticipation of something extraordinary about to happen. In the late morning when Forsythe brought her the Duke of Quill's card and said he was waiting in the front room, she was not surprised. In some remarkably clear and almost frightening way, Rose had known he would come and knew that he had done so specifically for one of two reasons. It would not take much conversation for her to determine which of the two it was. She straightened her collar and rearranged the pretty lace fichu she wore over her shoulders before she went downstairs. I am gathering courage, she realized, in case what I hear is not what I want to hear.

When Rose entered the room, John was struck by how fresh she looked, how glowing, really. He wasn't sure what he had expected but his last glimpse of her had been of a dirty-faced woman in crushed skirts with wide eyes and cheeks too pale, perhaps from weariness, perhaps even from fear, although he thought the latter possibility unlikely. Rose was the most fearless person he knew, man or woman, and he supposed that was one of the many reasons he loved her. She was convinced with all her heart of the power of right and similarly outraged at the wrongs of life. Her moral intuition was uncompromising and true. He thought she would at times be uncomfortable to be around but that she would never be simpering or dull and that suited him very well. *She* suited him very well. John had been completely certain he loved Lady Rose Carlisle the moment he wrapped both arms around her last evening and drew her close against him. She fit so perfectly in his arms that her body seemed to have been made solely for his embrace. Even under the duress of the moment, he had not wanted to let her go, not ever. If he had not been in danger of suffocating Evie, they might still be standing in that black and stinking hallway, his arms holding Rose close to his heart and his lips against her hair. He had wanted to keep her there forever. The memory of the moment was as vividly clear now as when it had occurred the day before.

Rose came into the room with both hands outstretched, eyes sparkling, and her wonderful smile turned fully on him. A sight to behold. Carmine slid in quietly behind her mistress.

"Your grace," Rose said with no repeat of her recent and comfortable use of his first name. With her greeting, his grace discovered he was sick to death of titles. *John*, she had called him yesterday and the small intimacy of his name on her lips had pleased him all out of proportion to the gesture. "I'm pleased to see you well," Rose went on. "Did your friend Inspector Bertram handle our malevolent Rat Catcher?" She motioned him to be seated and sat down herself across from him. Carmine took an unobtrusive place in the corner.

"Yes, he is incarcerated. If he does not hang, he will spend the rest of his life in the confines of Her Majesty's custody, but if ever there was a villain worthy of hanging, it's he, as unpleasant a piece of work as I have had the misfortune to meet. Bernard said he's trafficked in children for years."

John had come specifically to say something to Rose, had thought of nothing else throughout the night hours and thus, unlike Rose, had not slept well or awakened refreshed.

Rose, with the sixth sense she had developed about the man—when or how that had happened she didn't know—threw a look over at Carmine and asked, "Carmine, would you go see about refreshments for his grace and then please check on Cousin Alice, as well? I believe she was going to inventory the kitchen today and may need help."

Carmine, at first ready to object, took one look at the faces of the two people in the room with her and stood without protest. She supposed that since her young lady had wandered all over the east end of London by herself wearing disguises, had crouched in doorways and confronted murderous criminals, being alone with a man for a few minutes in her own front parlor was by contrast the height of innocence and safety. It was the duke, after all, and anyone with eyes could see that he would never do harm to Lady Rose.

"Yes, Miss."

"Oh, and Carmine."

"Yes, Miss."

"I believe I heard that Alice will need Forsythe's help in the pantry. You might find him and tell him to join her there immediately." A look passed between Rose and Carmine.

"Yes, Miss," Carmine said yet again and pulled the doors closed behind her.

Rose, still sitting, still smiling, smoothed her skirts and waited. She knew when she entered the room that the happy circumstance for which she had hoped would not occur, not today, anyway. Something was not right. John seemed troubled and intent on a course of action she was certain she would not like, but still Rose sat and smiled. She loved him, but she would not make it easy for him. As nonchalant as he appeared, one leg crossed comfortably over the other, impeccable in black—always so becoming to him, Rose thought with fond approval—and a crisp white shirt, she knew there was something churning inside him that he had come to say.

"Lady Rose, I wanted to come and make sure you were none the worse for yesterday's escapade."

"As you can see, I am quite myself. Thanks to you, of course, and Ernie, too. I shudder to think what would have occurred if Evie and I had met up with that monster of a man by ourselves."

"I believe he would not have stood a chance," John said—with Rose safely ensconced in her own front parlor, he could speak with dry humor of the predicament in which she'd found herself yesterday—"and while Ernie's credit is well earned, I did nothing but clutter up the alley."

"What nonsense! I think I have never been happier or more relieved to see anyone than when we collided in the hallway."

The same warm memory came to both their minds simultaneously, leading John to speak. "I have come to offer my apology for that particular incident."

"Apology?" Rose repeated the word with blank tone. "Why ever would you feel the need to offer an apology? You *rescued* us."

"I believe I over stepped and fear you might have considered my actions presumptuous and forward. It was the relief of the moment that caused my precipitous—"

His grace hesitated, unsure of the word to use and Rose filled in helpfully, "Embrace?"

"Well, yes, I suppose embrace would be as good a word as any to describe the, uh, the—"

"Embrace." Rose was helpful again. He frowned at her at that, catching something behind her mild tone that made him think that being helpful was not her primary motivation.

"Yes." Brief pause. "I fear I may have offended you by my familiarity."

Inwardly, Rose sighed. It was the unfortunate times in which they lived, she thought. There was always so much stuff and nonsense to get through and she was by nature impatient. Life was so very short.

"Not at all. Far from it, in fact."

"Far from it?" This time it was his turn to repeat words.

Rose, not a woman to equivocate, said, "I welcomed your embrace, John. Welcomed it with all my heart then and would welcome it now if you opened your arms to me." She spoke those amazing words with her hands folded in her lap and her clear blue gaze fixed on his face, watched a certain comprehension come into his eyes, saw a quick amazed happiness and then a shadow cross his face, saw it all in the space of a few seconds.

The conversation was not moving at all as he had planned and watching her gravely soft expression, John could not remember why he had thought it would. This woman in front of him, this Mrs. Greatheart, indeed, was like no other woman he had ever met. He had known that from the beginning and had been a fool to think she would be content with platitudes and proprieties.

"Lady Rose, you are very kind but—"

"Kindness has nothing to do with it, and if you continue to call me Lady Rose in that terribly correct voice you will force me to drastic action. Surely in the privacy of this room you could at least address me without the formality of a title. Now forgive my interruption. What were you saying?" The good doctor couldn't quite recall what he'd been saying but he forged on with admirable resolve.

"If not kindness, then perhaps it is gratitude you feel toward me, but I assure you that any gratitude would be misplaced and unnecessary, not that I don't appreciate your words in the spirit they were meant."

"I doubt that is true unless you are telling me that in the space of the last few minutes you have come to realize how much I admire you, how deeply you have engaged my affections, and how certain I am that if I do not marry you, I shall never marry at all. Is that what you are telling me?"

He could not respond. Warring inside John Merton was a great joy but a greater despair.

Rose, reading much of his inner turmoil on his face, went on, "I thought not. Like so many men, you are easily distracted by the distant future or the unfortunate past and completely blind to what stands right before you in your immediate present."

Caring for her as he did and wanting her happiness more than he had ever wanted anything in his life, John said quickly, "I don't think you ought to say any more. You will regret it."

"Will I?" Her tone was curious and nothing more. "Are you saying you feel nothing for me?"

He wanted to say just that, willed himself to say it, and opened his mouth to speak the words he had practiced. Instead of those desired words, however, he said, "No, I cannot say that."

"Good. We have made progress. Then if you care for me, John, even a little bit, why would you dissuade me from further speech and yourself from the freedom and happiness that come from reciprocated affection?"

"You don't understand."

"That is very true, probably the first really true thing you have said since you crossed the threshold today. Help me understand."

Rose's color was high, her cheeks flushed, and her eyes bright and brilliant. John thought she was the most beautiful thing he'd ever seen and loved her with a passion that made his chest ache, but as literate and polished as he was, an educated man who spoke three languages fluently and two more with colloquial smoothness, who argued with passionate persuasion in the House of Lords and was admired by the Queen, he could not find the words to explain. Perhaps because he himself did not fully understand.

Finally, he said with simple honesty, "I have never met a woman like you, Rose, or even imagined that one could exist. There is nothing about you that doesn't please me. If it were only face and figure that would be enough, but it is so much more. It is your character, your laughter, your kindness, your integrity, your passion, your unruly goodness. All those things please me and stir me. I had no idea I could feel like this, and I can't seem to take it in."

While she knew there was an unnamed obstacle still to overcome, his declaration answered Rose's question and completely satisfied her. There was much, much more than friendly admiration in his words and in his tone and on his face.

"So then, John, since we both seem to find the other acceptable, what is the problem?"

"I am the problem."

"You?"

"Yes." There was a cool misery in his tone that hurt her to hear. "I can't expect you to understand. I imagine it will all sound like foolishness to you, but I have never wanted anything as much as your happiness and you cannot have that with me."

"Forgive my thick headedness, but why exactly is that?"

"I have known for years, since boyhood, in fact, that I am not really loveable. I don't mean that in some kind of self-pitying way. It is simply a fact, a characteristic I possess the same as gray eyes and black hair. My ability to sustain deep and lasting affection in others, especially women, seems to be lacking in some way I can't quite fix, and I would not wish that for you, Rose. Of anyone in the world, you deserve a constant and continued happiness."

"What an extraordinary thing to say!"

Rose, an intelligent young woman, understood the meaning behind John's words and with the understanding came a great tenderness and a surge of love so strong she had to grasp the arms of her chair to keep herself from rising and grasping his lapels instead so that she could pull his head down to hers. All he needed, she reasoned, was to be soundly kissed and while she had limited experience with kissing, relegated to the unpleasant fumblings of youthful beaus, she thought she would do it anyway, as unpracticed as she was, and plan on figuring it out as she went along. Surely it couldn't be that hard. All sorts of people from milkmaids to royalty seemed to learn the art of kissing easily enough and from her parents she had noted an external technique that would at least get her started.

"It may seem so, I suppose, but I have given it a great deal of thought."

"Thinking of Lady Fountain, no doubt."

"Well, yes, partly. She was at first as impassioned as I about our union. She liked being with me, accepted my compliments and my attentions, protested her love on every occasion, anticipated the happy life we would have together, and then suddenly, abruptly, without a sign or word of warning she ceased caring for me." Rose stood at that, propelled by an inner energy that would not allow her to hear all this calmly.

"What dunderheads men can be! Let me assure you, John, that Lady Fountain's rejection of you had not one iota of personal animosity in it. She is as hard-headed and practical a woman as you are ever going to meet and when she compared Fountain's fortune and personal prospects to yours, you came in second. Your predilection for medicine was the deciding factor, I have no doubt. She never expected or intended for you to take her rejection personally. Let me guess. Even then—how many years ago was it now?"

"Seven."

"Seven!" The number seemed to overwhelm Rose for a moment but she finally continued, "Even seven years ago I would wager you had plans for setting up hospitals for the poor using your own wealth. I can see you as clearly as if I'd known you then, excited about medicine and the great opportunity, as you saw it, to contribute to the common good and make a difference in the world. Come now, John, stop romanticizing and admit that's true." He had risen, too, and they stood only an arm's length apart.

"Yes, it is true, but I thought she was of the same mind." Rose sighed at lost innocence.

"Of course, you did. You were young and lost in an idealistic haze, but I can tell you with the greatest certainty that your Penelope has never to this day had an idealistic thought in her entire life or for that matter an unselfish bone in her entire body. She was not about to share you and more importantly your fortune with the binding taskmasters of altruism and medicine."

Listening to Rose, John knew her words were true. He had not thought of Penelope exactly that way before, had always thought there was something in him which had disgusted her and which she had eventually come to despise, but remembering how he had last seen his faded love, remembering her recent words and the lines of discontent and selfishness that had disfigured her face, he felt as if the sun had suddenly come out from behind clouds. He had had little experience with women all those years before and finally realized that he had completely misread the incident and built up a mental fable around it, a self-indulgent, melodramatic fable.

"You may be right," he admitted. "I was every bit the callow youth then and my interactions with the opposite sex were limited to my cousin and her cousin, two admirable women. I suppose I thought all women were like Chloe and Abby."

With that acknowledgement, Rose knew she had surmounted one hurdle but with her recently acquired ability to see into his heart, she knew something else lingered there that would pose a much greater obstacle. Rose-like, she chose to meet it head on.

"Actually, I believe you thought Chloe and Abby and even Penelope were the exceptions, and that all women were really like your mother."

That she said it so baldly and in such an unemotional tone flabbergasted him. How could she have known and how dare she speak it aloud?

At the look on his face, Rose said urgently, "John, your father is no longer here forbidding you to speak of your mother and acting as if she never existed. It was unnatural for him to expect a little boy to participate in his bitter grief."

"As unnatural as a woman abandoning the son who worshiped her?"

"Yes, as unnatural as that. Neither parent had a care for your feelings."

"So explain my mother's actions as smoothly as you explained Penelope's. Do that if you can."

"I admit I cannot. My mother was so constant in our lives as children and is still so necessary to my father and to our family that I cannot imagine her leaving or picture our lives without her. But you don't know your mother's story or what caused her to take such an irrevocable step and while I confess I cannot pretend to understand how she could walk away without a backward glance, I am objective enough to realize that it can have nothing to do with you. To think that in some way you are responsible for that tragic occurrence is unreasonable, and surely as a doctor you must see that. If one of your patients came to you with this story, would you not say the same? You were hurt as a child but, my dear, isn't it time to put away childish things?"

As sincere as Rose was, as urgent and well-intentioned, the words were apparently the wrong words and a verbal misstep. His eyes cooled as she spoke.

"How refreshing to hear you admit that some things are beyond even your understanding, Lady Rose!"

His cool, slightly scornful tone stung, but with the self control she had learned and practiced through the years she did not retort in kind. Love stayed her tongue and her temper.

Instead, Rose said calmly, "Yes, and beyond yours, as well." She came to stand before him, stood slightly on tiptoe to kiss him firmly on the mouth, then walked past him to the door. He caught the familiar faint fragrance of lily-of-the-valley.

John regretted his chilly response as soon as he said the words but Rose's comments, as wise as they were, hurt, nevertheless and he had reacted instinctively to the pain. Now, the feel of her soft lips still fresh and her floral scent lingering lightly, he thought he would never be able to see the white, fragrant blossoms of lily-of-the-valley poke their heads out in spring without thinking of his Rose, a woman not to be deterred from what she believed was right, a woman both beautiful and practical. To him the perfect combination.

Rose paused before she opened the door to say, "Now I am the one who has over stepped. Please forgive me. It's clear you wish you were anywhere but here. You should know by now, however, that I never say what I do not mean. *I* am not inconstant and my family would be the first to tell you that I can be stubborn to the point of excess." John followed her into the hallway where Rose waited with his hat in her hands.

"My parents return from France in a week and I will return with them to Cornwall. If I don't have the happy opportunity to see you again, your grace, I wish you a pleasant life and a happy future." Her tone was politely conversational and nothing more.

John took his hat from her, frowning in the way she had come to recognize as a sign of deep thought. He would have said more but Forsythe came into earshot from around the corner of the hallway by the stairs and John could only nod and touch the brim of his hat in mute farewell.

No chance of a pleasant and happy life without you, my darling, he thought to himself, unsmiling, as he descended the front steps.

And a very pleasant and happy life we will have, my darling, Rose thought, smiling to herself as she ascended the stairs to her room. If you think I intend to return to Cornwall without you, you are gravely and monumentally mistaken.

Chapter 11

When Rose awoke the next morning, she did so with a cloak of resolve wrapped around her shoulders. She knew exactly what she must do and while she was somewhat unsure of the exact words to use, she had the general conversation mapped out in her mind already before breakfast.

Rose was at the morning table before her cousin and glanced up to smile at Alice as she fluttered in and say, "Now, cousin, don't tell me you have already been out and about at this early hour."

Alice blushed like a school girl. "I find I cannot sleep for thinking about Mayhew's return. I know that must sound foolish to a young woman like yourself, seeing me with thirty years of marriage, children, and grandchildren acting like an infatuated chit of a girl, but there you are. I confess it to you shamelessly." Alice's face was diffused with a pretty pink color and her expression was soft. Rose had never felt in such charity with her cousin as she did at that moment.

"It's not foolish in the least. I realize my parents aren't the only love match. Grandfather and Lady Margaret remain excessively happy, as do Uncle William and Aunt Abby, Uncle Matthew and Aunt Fanny, Aunt Cecelia and Uncle Harry—well, now that I think of it, the entire family." Alice, sitting down to coffee and toast, smiled.

"We've never given any thought to whether it's fashionable or not. Happy marriages and love matches just seem to run in the family." She watched a small smile play around the corner of Rose's mouth. "Isn't your sister Constance happy with her Reggie and doesn't your brother Robbie dote on his Helen?"

"Yes, to both, and Jamie will do the same one day, I shouldn't be surprised, only right now he's too busy being serious and pious. Father calls it a tedious habit and says he will outgrow it, but I think he's really quite proud of my brother's calling into the church. That any son of mine would take holy orders, Father says, is proof that God has a heightened sense of irony."

"Well, he's not far from wrong there," retorted Alice. "Your father was a rake and a heart breaker with ice water instead of blood running through his veins when it came to the ladies until he met your mother. The sound of him falling to earth rattled the china on the shelves."

That made Rose laugh, but she liked the idea of love matches running in the family. She intended to have one of her own.

"What are your plans for today, Rose?"

"I'm off to Madame Helene's for a new hat to replace that dear little chipped brim hat, which, alas, has disappeared."

"Disappeared? How could that have happened?"

"Carelessness, I imagine." Rose smiled as she spoke.

"More likely you gave it to some poor needy girl that caught your eye."

"I'd remember that, I think." For all her adventures, Rose remained careful never to tell a bold-faced lie when a half-truth would do. "And I shall stop by the Baroness's on the way home. She leaves on Monday for Lancashire—yes, I know, it seems to be a long leave taking—and since I am off to Cornwall soon, I don't know when we shall see each other again, if ever. I am sad to think of losing my new friend."

"But not the only new friend you made this spring," said Alice. "His grace, the Duke of Quill, seemed to enjoy your company." Rose raised her blue eyes to Alice.

"He did, didn't he?" she asked rhetorically and pushed away from the table. "I am not taking Carmine with me today, and,"—this as Alice began an objection—"please do not force me to act like a green girl just out of the schoolroom all the time. I will be five and twenty my next birthday, I have had more seasons than a calendar year, and I promise, truly promise, that I shall do absolutely nothing to compromise myself. I am very fond of both you and Carmine, but there are times I would like to go out without you hinting that if Carmine does not shadow me I will end up dancing through the streets clad only in my chemise."

"Rose!" But the picture made Alice laugh in spite of herself as Rose had intended and squelched whatever protest she might have made.

Rose's day progressed as she had outlined to Alice. She found a dainty straw hat with silk ties the color of raspberries and tiny little flowers of the same color perched along one side of the gently curving brim. It was perfect, she thought, eyeing herself critically in the glass, because the dress of white Corah silk she wore was covered in tiny polka dots of that same raspberry rose-red. She wore the hat as she exited the store, turning several heads as she did so, unaware of the picture she presented of a young woman in the full bloom of health and vitality with nothing frail or winsome or helpless about her. That might be what fashion dictated but by the looks several gentlemen sent after her, current fashion was not what appealed to the opposite sex. For her part, Rose was oblivious to glances of any kind, admiring from men or envious from women. She was a young woman with a plan and nothing was allowed to get in her way.

When she dropped the knocker on the Baroness's front door, Rose's heart was beating unnaturally fast and she was slightly breathless, yet when the maid opened the door, all she saw was a poised young lady. Rose greeted her in a pleasantly composed and thoughtful manner, shrugged off her shawl, and smiled at the Baroness's approach.

"You have just missed the children," the Baroness said, leading Rose into the parlor.

Although rented, the house had taken on the character of its inhabitant with elegant small porcelain figurines on the tables, chairs with turned, graceful legs and delicately brocaded seats, vases of flowers everywhere, and a picture on the wall from a new school of painters called Impressionists. Everything was light and cheerful.

"I sent them with Giselle to see the menagerie in Hyde Park. Evie was a little timid because this will be the first she has ventured out since that terrible man snatched her, but I assured her she would be safe. I sent Jean Paul along, too, and he is very, very big. Evie took one of his hands and Piper the other and both went off without a worry. Ernie, of course, could not be bothered to take anyone's hand. He is the *enfant terrible*, I think, and will always be so."

She sat across from Rose smiling as she spoke, a gray haired woman with soft brown eyes and a face lined by time or grief or hardship so that her age was hard to guess. Rose thought that all three had marked her and despite all she suspected could not dislike the Baroness, no matter how she tried.

"I did not come to see the children, Baroness. I came specifically to see you."

"And so I am here, Lady Rose, at your disposal." There was a brief silence, the Baroness examining Rose carefully, taking in the rosy bonnet and the rosier cheeks, the clear blue eyes under elegantly arched dark brows. "I think something has happened."

"Yes, something has happened and I need your help."

"Of course, if I can help, I will. Has it something to do with the children? You need not fear for them. I have become very fond of them, even Ernie, and I promise they shall be well cared for."

"It is not about the children, Baroness, or not about the three children you have so generously taken under your roof."

"Then what?" Rose took a deep breath.

"I find, Baroness, that I cannot bear the idea of life apart from the Duke of Quill. I had not imagined that I could feel this way, love so deeply or care so much. I suppose I thought there was no man right for me, no man who would not bore me after a week in his company, no man with whom I could share myself body, mind, and spirit, as marriage should be, as my parents' marriage is. I was always determined not to have less than they and I thought it would never happen. I know I am not the ordinary and I had accepted that, accepted the role of maiden aunt and eccentric spinster, but now—"

"Now the role has lost its appeal, no?"

"Yes. Completely and irrevocably."

"Do you think he does not reciprocate your affection?"

"Quite the contrary. I believe he loves me as desperately as I love him and perhaps even more so because he is so very alone while I have a large and boisterous family waiting in the wings."

"I agree with you, Lady Rose. I have seen the way his grace follows you with his eyes when he thinks no one notices. He is very correct, you know, and would not expose you to speculative gossip, but I sit on the sidelines and I watch his face when he thinks no one sees. For some time now he has had eyes only for you, ever since that meeting with the woman of the impossibly yellow hair." Rose said nothing so that the Baroness was finally forced to ask, "If your affection is reciprocated, how then may I help you?"

"John will not allow himself to love me, Baroness. He thinks there is only heartache in love and unfaithfulness and abandonment. He is afraid for me, he says, but I know it is more than that. I know he is afraid to love me because he believes he possesses some terrible flaw that will ultimately force me to leave him. He couldn't bear that again. He has not completely healed from the first time, you see."

"From this blonde woman, this Penelope, you mean?"

"Oh, no, Baroness. You know very well she was not the first woman that deserted him. You know that better than anyone."

Rose watched the older woman's face pale to the color of parchment. She appeared suddenly drawn and haggard and in some profound way so grief stricken that she looked twice her age. Rose, young and fearless and not willing to be in sympathy with the Baroness, felt her heart touched, nevertheless. There was so much pain in her, Rose thought, such restless pain. In a way it hurt to see it.

"I cannot imagine what you—" the Baroness began but with Rose's steady blue gaze on her stopped speaking abruptly. She took a deep breath before she spoke again.

"How could you know? There is no one alive who remembers me now. I was an only child and my parents are gone, and I lost all, even the most superficial, friends when I walked away from John's father. How did you guess?"

"It was the song."

"The song?"

"Yes." Rose sang the little refrain, slightly off key but recognizable. "'O, fish and fin and gill and scale / 'Twas the vision of a woman with a long green tail.' I heard John sing one verse of it to Evie when she first came to me and then later, after Evie came here, she sang an entirely new verse. When I asked her where she learned it, she said you taught it to her, that you came in every night and sang it to her, and I remembered that John once told me that his mother loved to sing, especially silly songs to make him laugh. I knew then." The Baroness's eyes were unnaturally bright.

"And now you despise me for what I did."

"I thought I might and I think I should, but I don't. I know you now as a generous woman who is kind to children and clearly you have experienced great grief in your life. I want to understand and I want you to make John understand so he can come to me with a free heart. He possesses such a great, grand heart that I realized I would not be content with just a broken part of it. I want it whole and I want it all."

"My dear Lady Rose, with your candid gaze and everything so uncomplicated to you, you cannot possibly understand."

"I can try. Let me try." Rose sat forward in her chair. "I don't want to live without him, and I believe you are the only one who can keep that from happening. I'll try not to judge. I just want to understand."

Coming to a decision, the Baroness began to speak.

"I was so young when I married, barely seventeen, very spoiled, very immature, the darling of doting parents, and the diamond of the season. Everyone was at my feet so when John's father offered for me, I was reluctant. There was no one else, but I loved the dancing and music and parties and late nights and laughter. Oh, I loved it all! My parents, however, desired the match and said it was best for me. A duke, they said, what an honor, and my father only a baron. I did not even like Leo very much, such a stiff and formal man, but I did as my parents wished and thought his great wealth would be enough."

"It was impossible from the start, living in that great, dark house with that great, dark man, so dignified, so concerned about the family name. I admit I never once thought of his feelings and now I believe he loved me in his way, but at the time, at the time…" Her voice faded, lost in memory, and then she resumed the story.

"John was born within the first year, a beautiful child, serious but with that wonderful smile. Mama this and Mama that, he would say, and hold his arms up to me wanting always to be picked up and cradled and sung to. For a while I thought the child would be enough, but his father said I spoiled him, said I would make him into a woman. He criticized everything I did. No singing, no laughing, no foolish games, he declared. None of that was proper for his son, the next Duke of Quill. He must be a man, ready to take his father's place, he said, and I was not allowed to spoil him."

The look on her face was so sad Rose could have wept. How unlike her own childhood with children running in and out of the bright rooms of Symonton Manor, with picnics and parties and Christmas puddings, *hide 'n find* and *duck, duck, goose*, with her mother as high-spirited as the children, skirts lifted and racing down the hallways and her father laughing at the sight, loving his Claire! Nothing dark or formal or harsh in the whole place. Every child treasured; every person loved.

The Baroness continued in her quiet, sad voice. "So it was natural, I suppose, that I should fall in love with the young man Leo brought in to tutor John in the classics. Not right, I never said that," the Baroness replied to Rose's unspoken affront, "but natural. Geoffrey was educated and literate, a handsome young man, younger even than I, a poet and a musician, and he loved me desperately, was always begging me to run away with him. Finally I could not say no. He was so bright and gay, everything Leo was not, and I had been miserable for ten years. It was the worst mistake of my life and I can blame no one but myself. I left my beautiful son behind, but I considered him lost to me already, and I knew his father loved him. John would want for nothing. Leo would be sure he had the best of everything his whole life. I was dying inside and could not bear to stay any longer, but I would not take John with me. I knew what I was giving up but I would not force my son to give up his birthright. I was selfish but not that selfish. So I sang good night to him that last night and after he was asleep, I packed my jewels and all the money I could find and left that dark place. I had been so sheltered, how could I have known there were darker places in the world?"

During the Baroness's narration, Rose had felt transported back in time, felt the confining, dark, and echoing house, the negligent husband, the young tutor enamored of the beautiful and unhappy duchess. It was almost like some gothic novel, but, of course, it was not a novel at all and it had no happy ending.

"It is a pretty story, *ne c'est pas*?" The woman's tone was tinged with self-recrimination but when she looked at Rose's calm, sympathetic face and found nothing judgmental there, she smiled. "If that was the end of the story, it might be bearable, but there is more, and I think it is not suitable for your ears."

"You misjudge me, Baroness, if you think I am so sheltered and so innocent that I do not understand the terrible things people do to one another. I have held too many mistreated children in my arms to be shocked or offended."

"So you will hear it all, then? All right, you shall. We fled to Paris, Geoffrey and I, and even now I cannot imagine what I thought we would do. That young woman is a stranger to me, a rebellious, willful, selfish, and unhappy stranger. Did I believe we could live on love?" The Baroness shook her head at the foolhardiness of the idea. "I had never been poor in my life, never wanted for any physical thing, and now suddenly I was trapped in a small apartment with a young teacher who could barely earn a living, who wanted me to sell my jewels and help support us. Sell my jewels! That he would even suggest such a thing was repugnant to me. I expected to be supported in the comfortable way to which I was accustomed and it became clear to me that Geoffrey would never be able to do that. He was an ineffectual dreamer and I soon came to despise those qualities which I had at one time admired, which had at first seemed so romantic and attractive."

"I met a man in Paris, a rich man it seemed—his name is not important—and he courted me when Geoffrey was away looking for work. He was very skilled, very persistent and practiced, and I was eager to regain the luxury I had given up. We would wed, he promised, as soon as my divorce in England was final. I told Geoffrey I could not stay with him any longer, begged him to forgive me, and left him. Poor Geoffrey. I can still see him standing in the middle of our little apartment, begging me to stay and promising me the world, but I would not listen and I would not stay."

"Of course, you must know how the story ends. This wealthy man, this man who swore his love for me, who wanted a wife, he said, was not wealthy and did not want a wife at all. He wanted my – companionship, shall we say? – and even more importantly, he wanted my jewels. One morning I awoke and he was gone as was everything I possessed. Everything. I was beside myself. I went to find Geoffrey but he was gone, as well. I wrote to my parents more than once and begged their help. I told them I had nothing. How could I live? My father might have helped me but not my mother. She could not forgive me. I had shamed them, she wrote, and they had no daughter any longer. I was not to contact them again. Not ever. It was the last word I had from either of them."

Of all the Baroness related, it was that which shocked Rose the most. To know their only child was desperate and vulnerable and alone, even if it was of her own making, and still to turn her away was incomprehensible. Rose knew she could have been a pirate, a poisoner, the worst creature imaginable, and still her parents would have taken her in.

"By then it was the middle of winter, bitter and cold, and I lived hand to mouth, too proud to beg, too fearful to sell myself on the streets, moving from room to room if someone had pity on me and offered me a warm place for the night. Finally, I decided life was too hard, too much of a struggle, too lonely, and too cold. I was ashamed and in despair. I would remember my son and think he must never know what his mother had come to. He must never know what I had done and how I had lived. One cold morning it came to me quite clearly that the only way to find relief was to die, that it would be easy and then the struggle of my life would be over. I was so tired and I longed for rest with all my heart. I thought I could find broken glass on the street and draw the sharp edge across my wrists and perhaps along my throat and bleed into the snow and sleep and die. I knew it would be easy and, indeed, it was."

The Baroness pushed up the sleeves of her satin gown, rolled back the lace along the wrists and showed the scars there. Rose reached out to touch the faded red lines with gentle fingers. She had come prepared to admonish but at the sight of those marks she knew only pity.

"I am so sorry." Her voice broke.

"But, no, Lady Rose, this is not the end of the story. See, I am here. It was my Pierre that found me, found me bleeding in the snow, a miracle that he did, and he took me to his home and brought in nurses and was so kind, so kind, the kindest man I have ever known. Like the Good Samaritan in the story, he asked nothing from me, just opened his home and his heart to me. How could I help but love him? Here is his picture." The Baroness reached for a daguerreotype from the side table and eagerly passed it to Rose.

Rose saw a small, dark man, hunched and misshapen despite an attempt to hide his physical attributes by seating his deformed side in shadows. But, oh, the face of the man, Rose thought. What a wonderful smiling face, open and mischievous and unafraid and kind!

"He looks like a splendid man," Rose said, handing the small frame back.

"Yes, he was. More splendid than I could ever describe. He had had a terrible injury years before and spent so much time in pain, but he was not one to complain. Life is an adventure, Anna, he would say, and so it was to him."

"Anna?"

"Anna was my given name, but when I married Pierre, I put my past life away and became Juliana, Baroness de Anselme. I remained Anna only in private with my husband. My Pierre loved me with such honest and unguarded emotion that I could not help but love him in return. I ceased seeing the crooked back and the bent legs and the awkward gait and saw only his heart. We were very happy. I nursed him through his last illness gladly, gladly, and would have given him my own heart if I could have, my own breath. I owed him everything and thought I could not live without him."

"But, of course, you will live, he would chide me, and my darling so ill his breath came in gasps. Life is an adventure, he would say, and you must live as long as the good God gives you breath. The good God, he said, and meant it despite his twisted body and the racking pain. Always the *good* God." The Baroness touched her eyes with a handkerchief but smiled as she did so. "He was such a one, that man. I miss him every day. After Pierre was gone, I began to dream about my son night after night and knew I could not rest until I saw him. It was as if he were calling me again as he did when he was a little boy and had a bad dream. So I came to see what kind of a man he had become."

"No wonder you were shocked when you discovered that the doctor kneeling in the street over the little boy your cab hit was your own son! I saw it on your face."

"Shocked?! *Mon Dieu*! I was more than that. I was speechless, breathless, astonished, overjoyed. All the emotions ran through me when I saw him there, so like his father and yet so unlike him, compassionate and tender with the little boy and yet so strong. And a doctor! How he must have had to fight his father for that! I was proud to be his mother, as little as I had to do with his raising. And, of course, you were there with your plans and your diversions, such a confident young woman sure of what was right and so fearless. I was charmed and honored to be your friend." She ended with a sad and wistful tone. "Now what you must think of me!"

Rose's tender heart had been deeply affected by the woman's story.

"I am still your friend, Baroness, and your identity is safe with me. I came prepared to chastise and to blame you, but I cannot. I know what you did was wrong, but I cannot find it in my heart to reproach you now after all these years. Still," Rose's softer tone became brisk, "you must tell John the story exactly as you told it to me. He has a right to know. He is the dearest dunderhead and will persist in believing that love must always be painful, that he is cursed in some ridiculous way so that one day I am sure to stop caring for him and abandon him willy-nilly. You must set him straight. He will listen to you."

"He will hate me."

"He hasn't the ability to hate, Baroness. His heart is too big for that. All I know is that I am not returning to Cornwall without a declaration from him and my parents are due back in town at the end of the week, so I haven't much time. I have a plan."

"I am sure you do," the Baroness interrupted, laughing a little, "but this you must leave to me. You will make him very happy, I think, Lady Rose."

"When I am not exasperating him enough to call me an idiot."

"He did not do so ungentlemanly a thing!"

"He most certainly did, but he meant it in the best possible way and he was right, besides."

Rose had a quick, vivid memory of being held tightly against John's chest, his arms wrapped around her and his hands in the small of her back, remembered his breath against her cheek, saw him lazily step between her and the Rat Catcher, one arm pushing her behind him for protection. The Baroness, watching the light color creep up Rose's cheeks, felt a rush of affection for this straightforward young woman. She was so exactly right for her son, would be the light and the love of his life, would never cease to delight him and would keep him young as Pierre had done for her.

"Life," the Baroness stated simply, "is its own adventure."

The opportunity for the Baroness to meet with her son came more quickly and more abruptly than either woman had anticipated. Rose, draped in a large plaid shawl of raspberry red and green, stood just inside the front drawing room bidding her hostess farewell after their recent, serious discussion when the knocker thudded against the front door.

"Monsieur Doctor," said the little maid at the door. There was a male murmur in response to the greeting. "But, of course, I will tell Madame you are here. Please do come inside."

Rose reached out a hand to squeeze the Baroness's arm.

"You will be fine. It is for his good and surely you see it is the right thing to do." The Baroness, too pale, could only nod.

John had somehow missed seeing Rose's carriage on the street and thus had not expected to meet her there. She looked as delectable as a summer picnic, wearing white and red and green with a little bonnet whose only assignment was to try to hold down some of her curls, a task at which it failed delightfully.

"Am I interrupting?" he asked at the sight of the two women standing shoulder to shoulder.

"No, not at all," Rose answered cheerfully. She might never have kissed him or told him she would have him or no man at all and he might never have stumbled over his words of admiration and given too much away. They had been bred, those two, for impeccable manners. "I was just departing. Have you come to say your farewells, too, your grace? Our friend, the Baroness, leaves for Lancashire at the end of the week."

When you leave for Cornwall, John thought sadly, and for a moment it seemed to him that all the light faded, inside and out, and that even the sun dimmed.

"Yes," he said. "I thought I would say good-bye to the children, as well. You will have your hands full, Baroness."

"Oh, no, no, no. They are refreshing, these children. I feel half my age when I am with them and we will deal very comfortably together on the trip, I assure you. Come, your grace, and sit down a while. I would like to talk with you."

"If you're sure I am not interrupting."

"I am certain you do not interrupt. Lady Rose and I have had a pleasant visit but she is off to break hearts, I am sure, as she looks so charming. Do you not think so?" Rose waited for his response.

"Yes, very charming." Rose was satisfied with his tone that held just the right mixture of stiff propriety and desolation and heartfelt yearning.

In the carriage on the way home, she felt she was as content as she could ever be without John by her side. She had done all she was able and had set wheels turning in what she hoped was the right direction. Now she must wait.

With a little catch in her heart, she spoke very softly as the carriage bumped along the cobbled streets. "I will wait for you, my dearest, until I am old and gray, but I hope it doesn't take that long."

Life may be an adventure exactly as the Baroness said, but it was also alarmingly short and Lady Rose Carlisle was far from a patient woman.

Chapter 12

After Rose left, John, trying to ignore the faint scent of lily of the valley that lingered in the air, seated himself comfortably across from the Baroness. She was very still and he thought too pale.

"Are you well, Baroness? Despite your protestations, I fear that having three active children suddenly thrust upon you has taken more of a toll on your health than you are willing to admit."

"Oh, no, your grace. I am very well and enjoy every minute of the children's company. I mean that quite sincerely, but even if it were not true I would never dare disappoint Lady Rose. She does not have much patience with an overly delicate nature and would soon set me straight. In her usual competent and kind way, I am sure, because there is nothing rag-mannered about her. Do you not agree?" He nodded, not wishing to speak of Rose to anyone, even to this woman who had been in on the adventure from the start. "I have wanted to speak to you, your grace, for some time, for a longer time than you can imagine." At that point John was curious and nothing more.

"Of course, Baroness. Is this in a medical capacity?"

"No, no." He had been certain it was a medical ailment of some kind that she wished to discuss and was taken aback at her vigorous denial.

"Then what? If there is something I can do for you, some service I can offer, you need only ask."

"That is very kind of you, kinder than I deserve. I wish to speak to you about mistakes."

"Mistakes?" he repeated, puzzled.

"Yes, mistakes; certainly mine and if you are not careful, perhaps yours as well. You volunteered a service and I have something to ask of you." At her words and tone he had grown more than curious, was now expectant and oddly, almost anxiously, anticipatory.

"What may I do for you, madam?" he asked quietly.

Her eyes were very bright as she answered, "I ask you to listen. Promise that you will listen through all of my speaking. You need say nothing, only listen until I finish. Will you promise to do that?"

"Of course. That is easy enough."

"Not so easy as you think to hear my story, but if you are ready—" He settled back in the chair.

"I am. Feel free to speak whenever you choose. I promise to listen."

And so at his invitation, she began the sad story of a foolish young woman and a lost little boy.

Later, when the telling was done and afternoon shadows had lengthened in the room, the two people there, the gray-haired woman and the gray-eyed man, sat in silence. The parlor door had opened briefly, Giselle back with the children, but the Baroness had given a quick, vehement shake of her head and the door had quickly closed again. The silence in the room lengthened.

"I don't know what to say," John finally admitted. From the beginning, once he had recognized the enormity of the story, he had kept his gaze fixed steadily on the Baroness's face, studying every line, every movement, every expression.

"You need not say anything, my dear boy. I fear it is too late for words as much as I wish that were not so."

Looking at her now and knowing what he did, it was obvious to him that the Baroness was exactly who she said she was. He could see it in the small dimple in her cheek, in her lustrous brown eyes, in the small, ineffectual gesture she had always had that he just now recalled of brushing her hair away from her face. All these years and here she sat in front of him. Through his adolescence John had wondered in his very private thoughts how he would act if such a reunion ever took place, if she were alive despite his father's hints to the contrary. One moment he thought he would be scornful and accusatory, the next cool and nonchalant, but now that it had actually happened, he felt none of those things.

His heart was constricted with an emotion that to his utter astonishment he recognized as joy. She should not have left but he knew, better than anyone, how dark and empty and cold that great house could be, how dark and empty and cold his father had been for a long time, too. Even at the end of his life, mellowed with age and humbled by ill health, the elder Quill had been a proud man, not one to compliment or cosset, with nothing tender or comforting about him. He had loved his son but affection had been hard for him and the sharing of affection harder still. John had loved his father, too, despite everything, but there had been many times he had not liked him very much.

The Baroness started to reach out a hand to John, pulled it back into her lap with an effort, and finally said, "I would have gone to my grave not telling you. What can it serve, I thought, but to stir up feelings of anger and bitterness in you? I planned to let the dead stay buried, but Lady Rose would have none of it."

"She knows?" John was incredulous.

"Do you not realize by now that she knows everything?" Mother and son shared their first smile in twenty years.

"But why should she—?"

"Listen to me, John, because this is one thing of which I am certain. If you are loved, you have been given a great gift. There is none greater. So many people go through their lives without that grand adventure, as my Pierre called it, but it need not be so with you. Your Lady Rose is as true a woman as you will ever find and she will bring you more joy than you can imagine. Oh, my dear, dear boy, you will regret it until the day you die if you let her go out of your life. I know something of love but even more of regret and I say to you take the chance, John. Life is short and some things can never be forgiven or undone." Two large tears pooled at the corners of her eyes, spilled over, and began to trickle down her lined cheeks. Without thinking, her son bent forward and with his handkerchief gently wiped away the tears. She did not move but sat still as stone.

"It's true," he told her, "that some things cannot be undone, but there is nothing that cannot be forgiven." Then he stood and taking her scarred wrists in his strong hands pulled her to her feet. He put both arms around her and, the roles of parent and child reversed for that moment, said with tender comfort, "Don't cry. It will be all right. Don't cry, Mother," the name sweet to speak but sweeter still to hear.

There was more that needed to be said, certainly, but it would take time. Later they would talk about the past again and the future, as well, but not just then. The Baroness was suddenly exhausted and John had any number of things to consider, many of them having to do with distant Cornwall and a young woman with clear blue eyes and a taste for adventure.

After a quick and preoccupied evening meal at home, John sat with a snifter of brandy before the fire thinking well into the night.

On his way up to bed, he said cheerfully to his old and faithful retainer, "What do you think about change, Rathbone?"

"There is a time and place for it, your grace." Rathbone was cautious in his response because he wasn't quite sure where the conversation was headed. John gave him an uncharacteristic thump on the shoulder on his way past him up the stairs.

"You are absolutely right, old friend, though we haven't experienced much change of late, have we?"

"No, your grace."

Halfway up the steps, Dr. John Merton, fifth Duke of Quill, began to whistle a jaunty tune stopping mid-melody long enough to call over his shoulder, "Then I think it's time we did. Past time, in fact. Change is good for the soul, Rathbone, and life is an adventure, after all."

He reached the first landing and Rathbone, listening from below, heard the whistle change to a song sung in the duke's pleasant baritone. He couldn't quite make out all the words and what he heard sounded like a bit of foolishness: *O fish and fin and gill and scale / something something woman with a long green tail.* He heard the duke singing to himself until the door of his room closed and abruptly shut off the sound.

Change, was it? the old man asked himself. Not hardly. It wasn't the idea of change that made his master sing, it was a woman, for sure. He couldn't have been happier for the duke, a good and honorable young man that had been alone for too long, and both the house and the man would blossom under a woman's touch. Rathbone didn't much care about the woman's background or parentage or physical appearance or reputation. He only hoped, at the risk of being indelicate, that the new duchess would have two normal human legs. Otherwise he'd be hard pressed to know what to do with that long green tail.

That same night, Rose had an uncharacteristically difficult time falling asleep. She had tried to stay occupied that afternoon and each time her mind had veered toward the elegant little sitting room in the Baroness's elegant little house, she had forced herself to think of something else. That particular meeting and conversation were not for her ears and not fodder for speculation. It was too personal for both the Baroness and John and certainly painful for both, too. But try as she might, Rose could not help herself. It was not so much what John's reaction to his mother's story would be. Of that Rose was certain. He was the kindest man she had ever met and noble in a way that had nothing to do with title and ancestry. He would hear the Baroness's sad history and the regret in her voice, would see the grief on her face and the scars on her arms, and he would take her into his heart without a thought. Dr. John Merton, fifth Duke of Quill, was not a vindictive man and would not hold a grudge. His rational good nature was one of the reasons Rose loved him.

What she wondered about, what made her restless and unsettled, was how it would affect his feelings for one Lady Rose Carlisle. For the first time in her life Rose experienced self-doubt and she didn't much like it. What if she had read his feelings wrong? What if she had been presumptuous? What if he didn't care for her as she suspected? Rose was so unused to such miserable, shaken self-confidence that she turned from side to side in bed, punching the pillow and muttering to herself until she finally sat up, thrust her feet into her slippers, wrapped her dressing gown around her, and stole downstairs to the library. The last time she'd been unable to sleep in the middle of the night she had met a fearful villain in the hallway but this time there were no intruders. No children asleep in the big bedroom, either, no plan to be concocted, nothing to challenge her intellect, and no one to outsmart. Very plainly, no adventure. Life was boring and dull and she felt abjectly sorry for herself.

Once in the library, Rose lit a lamp and picked up the first book she found sitting out on the desk. The Farmington family Bible. She wondered if that was Alice's doing and if her cousin was more lonely and worried about Mayhew on foreign shores than she admitted. Rose fingered the parchment pages of the old, leather-bound book. She supposed she should start getting used to reading the Scriptures on any and every occasion, morning, noon, and night and at every meal besides, because she was undoubtedly destined to be the old maid sister keeping house for her saintly brother Jamie, renowned high church parson and writer of scholarly sermons. The picture of the two of them, gray-haired and reverent over matins and vespers, over breakfast devotions and supper readings made her grimace.

Despite her continued searching, nothing of interest leaped out at her from the library's shelves. Rose sighed. She should just go back to bed and count something, sheep or maybe lost opportunities, and perhaps sleep would eventually come. She placed the old Bible back on the desk and for no reason glanced down at the pages spread open there. A few words caught her attention and Rose began to read more intently. After a moment she dropped into the nearest chair and pulled the entire book into her lap. Now whole-heartedly absorbed in the text, she gave a happy little murmur of laughter as she read, a sound of joy in the dimly-lit room, a sound of satisfaction and wonder and almost triumph.

"'Thou shalt number seven sabbaths of years unto thee, seven times seven years,'" Rose began and read the whole chapter, comforted by the grand picture of restoration and belonging, of leaving the past behind and starting fresh again, of prisoners freed and debts forgiven, and of returning to one's true family after difficult times. *He shall go out in the year of jubilee, both he, and his children with him.* Rose thought about release and celebration and said the word *jubilee* aloud into the dark library one final time before she closed the big book, snuffed out the lamp, and went upstairs to bed where she slept dreamlessly well into the morning.

John awoke at his usual hour, intending to be off to his surgery for the morning followed by enormous plans for the afternoon. He surprised his valet when he shook his head in disapproval at the clothes set out for him.

"But, your grace," said Bellevue, "you always prefer a sober look."

"Do I?" John stared in frowning concentration at the well-pressed black pants, the black suit coat, everything professional and unremarkable. "Well, not today. What can you do for me today, Bellevue? Don't turn me into a harlequin, of course, but can you not add a little color somewhere. What about this?" He pointed to a morning coat hanging forlornly in the wardrobe amidst so much black, a lustrous gray with the tiniest fleck of black tweed. "Why haven't you ever allowed me to wear this? It's a very nice fabric, isn't it? Or is it hopelessly out of fashion? For all I know it could be, I suppose."

Bellevue gaped at the duke in amazement, then hastily took out the coat and its lighter gray trousers, very modish and sure to be handsome on the duke with his gray eyes and black hair.

"No, your grace, it is the height of fashion and I have tried on more than one occasion to get you out of the black of which you are so fond. Not that black doesn't look handsome on you, your grace, but it is nearly summer and this would be just the thing. Not for the surgery, you always say. Black is what patients want to see, you always say. Well, praise be to whatever conversion you have experienced!" Before John had a chance to change his mind, Bellevue whisked away the usual black and brushed and set out the lighter gray. Flicking a non-existent speck from John's shoulder, the valet casually added, "Is it some special occasion today, your grace? I beg your pardon if I've forgotten," knowing full well he'd forgotten nothing of the sort. John smiled to himself at the question.

"It is not a special occasion yet, Bellevue, but I believe it could be. No, I believe it definitely will be." That said, he was down the stairs and reaching for the front door handle still whistling—his grace had been whistling nearly all morning—as Rathbone caught up with him.

"Should we set supper for you this evening, your grace?"

John did not answer immediately. Instead he asked a question of his own. "Do you remember my mother, Rathbone?" If the old man was taken aback at the unexpected inquiry, he didn't show it.

"It has been twenty years, your grace, but yes, I remember the duchess very well."

"Good. Good. How's your heart, Rathbone?" Rathbone kept pace with the conversation.

"Sound, your grace. You'll recall that you gave me a look over earlier this year and pronounced me fit."

"That's right, I did. I wanted to be sure. I wouldn't want anything sudden, a surprise visit from someone you didn't expect, say, or a change to our living arrangements to unsettle you and cause problems for your heart."

Oh, it's not *my* heart that's the problem, thought Rathbone in response to this insensible speech, but he said aloud, "That's very considerate of you, your grace."

But that was too much, even for John in his present euphoric state and he laughed out loud.

"You are a patient old friend to tolerate my rambling. No, no supper tonight, but I will have guests tomorrow, at least two people, and it should be special, very special, as special as the guests themselves." The doctor went off to his surgery in a splendid gray suit and a cheerful blue handkerchief peeking out of the breast pocket, saw patients, instructed new mothers, listened good-naturedly to the ailments of old women, peered into ears and throats, and dandled babies, humming all the while.

Rose waited at her cousin's house all morning and well into the afternoon and while she wasn't sure for what she waited, she certainly knew for whom. By mid-afternoon he had not come and conveniently forgetting that he was a doctor with a thriving practice of people who prided themselves on having a duke for a physician, Rose began to imagine the worst. He was upset that she had interfered in his personal life and would never speak to her again. The meeting with the Baroness had gone poorly and he was even now wishing it had never happened, wishing Rose to the devil for her managing ways.

Finally, she stood abruptly from her contemplation of the library globe and said, "Please come along, Carmine. I cannot bear the continents or this house any longer and I would appreciate the company, if you don't mind."

Carmine had watched Rose surreptitiously, more concerned than she let on. Truth be told, she missed skulking through hallways and creeping up stairs and hiding food trays under pillows. There hadn't been an adventure in quite a few days and life had become dull and monotonous. It wasn't at all like her Lady Rose and Carmine was worried so the idea of an outing was welcome.

"Where are we bound, Miss?"

"Farmer and Rogers in Regent Street," Rose answered decisively. "I am in the mood for a new shawl and a little one for our Evie, too, something in sunshine yellow as a going away gift."

Once there, Rose got down to business and found the perfect shawl for herself to match her dress of soft bluc Chambertine sprigged with darker blue cornflowers the exact color of her eyes. She had just purchased a dear little shawl and bonnet for Evie, pleased with the picture of the little girl's delight as she opened the package, when someone spoke Rose's name. Looking up, Rose met Chloe Fitzhugh's smiling gaze.

"Lady Rose, how very nice to see you! I have wanted to tell you how pleased I was that you attended our little party recently. Charles and I felt honored."

"I was the one honored to be invited."

The two young women, recognizing similarities in the other that made her instantly sympathetic and likeable, conversed easily. Rose thought she would have liked Chloe even if she wasn't John's cousin. Chloe had a similar feeling about Rose for a somewhat similar reason. If they became cousins-in-law, it would be welcomed by both.

Their easy conversation was interrupted by the clear and too loud sound of a woman's laugh nearby, a grating trill that started up the musical scale and stopped just before it reached full octave—Penelope Carstairs, Lady Fountain, the woman whose hair owed more to artifice than to nature and whose smile never quite made it to her eyes.

That is all I need, thought an annoyed Rose. She recognized the unpleasant laugh immediately but continued the conversation with Chloe without displaying a whit of aggravation in either her tone or expression.

Yet when Rose heard Lady Fountain say in her carrying voice, "Your grace. John," she turned despite being taught never to stare and saw John Merton scanning the crowd of shoppers. The man seemed intent on one objective and was not about to be bothered or distracted by anything not in keeping with his goal.

Rose saw John before he saw her. He looked very fine in fashionable gray and she considered the lighter color an omen of sorts and a sign of a lighter heart even as she admitted to herself that she might be reading too much into her beloved's fashion selections. To her delight and uncharitable satisfaction, Rose watched John nod briefly to Lady Fountain in passing, realized that he did not even recognize her, and felt a soaring and perhaps unflattering happiness. Lady Fountain looked flabbergasted, reached out a hand to grab his sleeve, and missed. It's over, Rose thought with relief and was distracted from the delightful realization when John's gaze finally found her in the crowd. For one moment it seemed that everyone in the place either melted away or suddenly ceased talking and became motionless.

Then he stood before them saying to Chloe but with eyes only for Rose, "Hello, cousin."

Chloe, an intelligent young woman with a devoted husband of her own, recognized the signs and taking Carmine's arm said, "Goodness, John, I can't remember the last time I've seen you out shopping." She gave Carmine a persistent pull, saying as if she always went shopping with other women's lady's maids, "Come over here and look at this. I think it's perfect, don't you?" Carmine, not as well-born but just as smart in her own right, did not resist.

"Is it serendipity that you came upon us here, your grace?" Rose asked.

"Serendipity!" John made a sound unworthy of a duke. "I went to your cousin's house and when I discovered you weren't there, I browbeat Forsythe into telling me where you had gone. It was my purposeful intent to find you and serendipity may have none of the credit. And I would sincerely appreciate it if you would stop calling me your grace. You've called me John on more than one occasion and I like the sound of it. Couldn't you call me just plain John?"

"That seems rather wordy, doesn't it, Just Plain John? If it's agreeable to you, I'll shorten it to Plain John." She spoke seriously but her eyes twinkled. The corners of his lips twitched in return.

"You may call me anything you wish, Plain John or Just John or Just Plain John, but on occasion I would prefer *my dear* or *my darling*. Anything from your lips is fine, however. I find I am entranced by your lips in general, by the way. They are quite delectable."

Rose gave a little gasp at the way his eyes lingered on her mouth, looked around, and said in a lowered voice, "Thank you." Recovered, she added in a more normal tone, "How are you after your meeting yesterday? Is everything well?"

Her concern was so genuine and her blue eyes so warm that if he hadn't thrust both hands into his pockets, he would have scooped her up and kissed her right then and there.

"Everything is very well, thank you. It's more than I can comprehend right now, but because of you I believe that particular story will have a happy ending." People began to move around them again and the queer stillness that seemed to envelop them lifted.

"I'm so glad, so very glad. I knew you were too good to be vindictive or want to punish her for the heartache she caused."

"Punish her? If her cab hadn't knocked over Piper, I would never have met you. That more than makes up for anything else. The past is just that and I have no intention of repeating my father's poor, cold, lonely life. I have been a foolish and fearful man, Rose, and I ask you to forgive me. You told me once that you would welcome my affections and if that is still the case, I am here to offer them."

His speech had the effect of making her heart begin to beat very fast and then move up somewhere toward the base of her throat. John took a step closer so that he could have easily reached out to touch her, but when he moved to take her hands in his, she stepped back and held up one hand to ward him off.

"Are you making an offer for me, John, right here in the middle of the Farmer and Rogers shawl shop?"

He looked about at the customers trying not to listen and at Chloe doing her best to shoo the people around them in other directions.

"Yes, I think I am. How is one supposed to do it? Your father is in Paris and I expect I should ask him first and honestly, my darling, if this is making you uncomfortable, I will wait and do just that. Or we could go some place private if you prefer, but be assured that making an offer in a shawl shop does not bother me in the least."

Carmine, overhearing because it was impossible not to, had a fleeting, hopeful thought that her young lady would take the duke up on his suggestion and adjourn at least to a back room, which might afford some degree of privacy, but even as the thought crossed her mind she sighed. She really must give up on the idea that her Lady Rose was ever going to do anything with the decorum appropriate to her station. Not that Carmine minded all that much, since it had been so boring of late and it would make a wonderful story for the children someday.

"Yes," she would tell them as she tucked them into bed, "I was there when your father proposed to your mother, right there in the middle of the finest shawl shop on Regent Street, people milling all around and trying their best not to notice." Smiling to herself, Carmine turned her back to the couple and pretended to be interested in a display of kid gloves.

Arm still outstretched palm forward, Rose said sternly, "I cannot allow you to continue, John. I am convinced that you are overwhelmed by the reappearance in your life of one you held in great affection and you feel a natural, a very natural, gratitude for the small part I played in the reunion. You have not given this enough thought." If he was astonished by this sudden change of attitude in his darling, he didn't show it.

Instead, he folded his arms across his chest and said with warm tolerance, "I assure you that this conversation is not about gratitude and I have given my decision more thought than you can know, many sleepless nights and distracted days of thought." Rose vacillated.

"Well, that's all right then, but I believe you are still laboring under certain illusions about me, and I won't come to you under false pretenses."

Trying not to smile, John said, "My dear, I wish you would believe me that I have absolutely no illusions about you. Not a one."

Rose couldn't decide if she should be relieved or insulted and continued in a rush, "You should know that I can't sew a stitch or sing a note on key and while I was given art lessons by a very reputable teacher, I am simply awful. I couldn't paint a recognizable object to save my soul. As to temperament, I am exactly like my mother only worse, a managing female that likes to have her own way. I am impatient and I absolutely cannot tolerate unkindness or bullying. I sometimes act without thinking and you know that I enjoy hatching hare-brained schemes. I have seriously embarrassed every member of my family at least twice."

At her pause for breath, he interjected, "Are you done now?"

Rose shook her head and went on, "I am not at all the fashion and I never will be. I haven't a meek bone in my body and I won't necessarily agree with you on everything. I shall always love you, but I have no doubt we will have to muddle through disagreements now and then. I am not fair and pale and quiet. My hair is dark, my complexion ruddy, and as you can see I am hopelessly beetle-browed." She began forthrightly enough but ended with an almost shy smile and an uncharacteristic diffidence. "That said, if you're certain you want such a creature, she is yours, but you must take me as I am and at your own risk. There. Now I'm done."

Lady Rose stood before him oddly vulnerable, with her eyes bright and a proud thrust to her chin and John laughed out loud, came to her, put both arms around her, and pulled her close. She fit, as she had once before, exactly right in his arms, as if they had been made for each other and tailored to the other's contours.

"I do want you," he told her in a low voice, "now more than ever and God willing every day more than the day before. I agree to it all and I want to seal the contract." Then he proceeded to kiss her, thoroughly, publicly, and for a very long time. Later, her cheek against his jacket, he heard her give a low chuckle.

"What?" he demanded and she answered in a muffled but thoughtful voice, "I knew kissing couldn't be all that difficult to learn and that I'd be able to figure it out as I went along. I was right, too, but I had no idea it was so enjoyable. I think there's room for improvement, however, and more practice would be in order. Don't you agree?"

Standing in the middle of the most exclusive shawl shop on Regent Street, Dr. John Merton, fifth Duke of Quill, smiled down into Lady Rose Carlisle's clear blue eyes. The look she saw there, a wondrous combination of tenderness and pride, humor and a humbling fierce protectiveness, had an odd effect on her chest. Something—was it love?—had begun to flutter around inside her with alarming vitality.

"You know," the duke drawled, setting her away from him and reaching to tuck a stray curl back under her little hat, "you make a very good point, my darling. It's a capital idea and I wish I'd thought of it myself. Would you like to join me for a ride through the park?"

Casting caution to the winds and with a complete disregard for her reputation, Rose tucked her hand under his arm and gave him a glowing look.

"What a lovely idea!"

They walked out together, past the smiling face of Chloe Fitzhugh who loved her cousin John and thought that he had finally found a life partner to make him happy, past an expressionless Carmine who was already dressing Rose for the wedding, and past the disdainful Lady Fountain, who had given a gasp, more from offended pride than moral outrage, at the sight of Lady Rose Carlisle in the arms of the Duke of Quill. Lady Fountain turned away as if the sight disgusted her but truth be told, it was not disgust that darkened her ladyship's expression but rather envy and a sudden, sharp regret. For all the suitors she had known, both before and after her marriage, and for all the fervent protestations of affection she had heard, no one, her husband included, had ever looked at her with anything close to the love and delight and pride that radiated from John Merton's face as he took Lady Rose Carlisle's hand.

John and Rose were oblivious to Lady Fountain, however, oblivious in fact to everyone there. Focused only on the other and each conscious of a wild, careening joy, the duke and his lady stepped out into the afternoon warmth, impatient to start their own adventure of a lifetime.

Epilogue

Several years later, Rose Merton, Duchess of Quill, stood in the broad doorway that opened from the library onto the stone verandah. The French doors were flung open to let in the fresh fragrances of the season. It was late June in Kent, green lawns and the gardens blazing with color, children tumbling over one another on the grass and chasing each other through the small maze of shrubs and rose bushes. The family dogs added to the hubbub with those peculiar short, sharp barks that indicate they are having the finest time of their lives and these are the best children ever! There was always an abundance of children wherever the Mertons resided, whether at their London town house or here at the family's country estate. Rose was never exactly sure where all the children came from, taken from orphanages, rescued from factories, snatched down from chimneys and up from the mines. She would have been hard pressed to give a count at any given time.

The duchess looked out at the horizon, watching and waiting. It was a clear day without a cloud anywhere and nothing to distract from the beauty of the countryside. The air was so crystalline that she had convinced herself she could see the hospital in the distance. The fourth Hospital of Mercy underwritten and funded by the combined Merton and de Anselme fortunes and supplemented with the duchess's substantial and well-invested Carlisle dowry.

"One hospital for each child we have," John had promised when they had joyfully discovered the news of a first child. "How can we endure such happiness when others live in misery and pain?" She had loved him very much at that particular moment, loved him even more now, four children and four hospitals later. A hospital for the poor in Lancashire, one in Kent, one in Cornwall, and one built over a block of razed buildings in the East End where once a little girl in a daffodil yellow dress sat cross-legged in the dark and comforted herself with a song about a mermaid.

Both John and Rose were recently awarded the Most Noble Order of the Garter by the Queen herself, given in appreciation for services to the nation, he a Knight Companion and Rose a Dame. Their families were proud, the two awardees embarrassed and somewhat discomfited. To be given a prestigious award for doing what one loved, what made one happy, didn't seem right but it would have been boorish to refuse. How does one say *no, thank you* to Her Majesty, after all? The ribbons were upstairs somewhere, in a bureau drawer, perhaps, or in Rose's jewelry box. If she ever had to lay her hands on them in a hurry, she would be in serious trouble.

One of the children on the lawn, spying Rose in the doorway, gave a shout and waved. Rose waved back but never took her eyes from the horizon where she was sure she caught a distant shadow and stir of dust. There, at last he came, returning to his property in fulfillment of their own private and perpetual year of jubilee. Rose could see the carriage clearly now. John was finally home after a too-long trip, a tour of all the facilities, a teaching stint in Cornwall, a lecture in Sussex, a visit with his mother—not to mention Ernie, Piper, and Evie besides—in Lancashire, gone much too long although she never begrudged him the time. His love of medicine was surpassed by only one greater love, each passion enriching the other, and she was content with the order of things.

The carriage pulled onto the drive from the road and moved out of sight as it took the graceful curve toward the front of the house. Rose relaxed, already feeling her husband's presence in the house. She heard the front door open, heard him call her name, heard his steps on the tile floor of the hall pick up speed.

"In here," she called and waited to hear the door open.

John came up behind his wife, put both arms around her waist, pulled her against him, and rested his cheek against her hair. He said nothing at first, only gazed out at the yard filled with the noise of children, content to have her in his arms. Rose leaned back against him, quiet, too.

He took a heady, deep breath of lily of the valley before he said quietly, "Hello, my darling. Is everything well with you and the children?"

"Yes, love. Except for missing you, we are all right as rain."

They stood a moment longer in silence until John asked, "Is it my imagination or has the number of children increased in the month I was gone?"

"It has increased, my dear, but only temporarily. Chloe's three have been visiting since last Saturday and Jamie sent his two on Tuesday. I've charged Carmine with maintaining a count and she seems to be keeping up so I'm fairly certain she would know if we misplaced any. I warn you, though, that I have heard troubling reports about Levorson's Mill two counties over and if Mr. Levorson does not improve the way he treats the children that work for him, I will need to appear in his doorway. If that happens, our ranks might swell briefly until everything is resolved. I have let the word trickle out that I may be forced to pay a visit and we can hope the man mends his ways."

"Or—"

"Or I shall be forced to create a scene, and you know how he would hate that."

"Were I Levorson I would be quaking in my boots."

Rose turned in her husband's embrace, looped her arms around his neck, and lifted her face to his, her eyes sparkling and as clear blue as the summer sky outside the windows.

"Indeed? And what exactly are you suggesting, Just Plain John? That I am a shrew and a termagant and a brawling woman?" She tried to give him a stern look but failed lamentably in the attempt.

John's arms tightened around her as he answered, laughter in his voice and something else there, too, a husky warmth and an appreciative, muted astonishment at everything that was his.

"I am suggesting that you, dear Jubilee Rose, are the most adorable woman of my acquaintance, the joy of my life, and the mother of my children, a woman I missed desperately every day of the last month and whom I shall always love to distraction." He brought his mouth very close to hers and whispered just before kissing her, “Even if you are hopelessly beetle-browed.” That caused a little explosion of laughter from her which was quickly forgotten in his insistent, passionate kiss.

As they held each other there on the verandah, oblivious to the scene they made and so close in their embrace that from a distance they could have been mistaken for one figure, two little girls sat with their backs against the opposite side of the verandah wall, warmed by the afternoon sun and chatting haphazardly. The girls were mirror reflections with clear blue eyes and hair as black as a raven’s wing, dressed in striped frocks, one in rose and one in blue, each with a white ruffled pinafore overtop. They were still children, round-faced and sweetly awkward, but their faces and figures held the future promise of beauty and grace. A lean white cat lay curled in the sunshine atop the brick wall behind them, completing the picture.

“Papa’s home, Anna,” said one.

“Yes,” responded Anna sensibly, “but he and Mama are occupied and you know we are not allowed to interrupt.” They sat quietly until Anna took her sister’s hand and began to sing in a childish but true soprano, “O, fish and fin and gill and scale.”

At which point her sister joined in, her tone not nearly as true since she had inherited her mother’s unfortunate ear for music but raising the volume enough to make their parents on the other side of the wall pull apart and look at each other with amusement.

“’Twas the vision of a woman with a long green tail.”

The song ended and as if on cue the two little girls threw their arms around each other and dissolved into happy, helpless, unstoppable giggles. Their papa was home and kissing their mama and all was right with the world.

If you enjoyed *Jubilee Rose* and have yet to read the first two books in The Penwarrens, don't stop here.

Read the back story of John Merton and his cousin Chloe in *Listening to Abby* and meet Lady Rose's parents, Robert, Marquis of Symonton and his wife, Claire in *Claire, After All.*

As Cousin Alice so accurately described, "Happy marriages and love matches just seem to run in the family."

Books by Karen J. Hasley

The Penwarrens
Claire, After All * *Listening to Abby* * *Jubilee Rose*

The Laramie Series
Lily's Sister * *Waiting for Hope* * *Where Home Is*
Circled Heart * *Gold Mountain* * *Smiling at Heaven* (2014)

and *The Dangerous Thaw of Etta Capstone*